KT-233-390

WITHDRAWN

X000 000 052 1873

ABERDEEN CITY LIBRARIES

This was crazy.

She'd just met the man, yet he did something to her that she couldn't quite put into words. Granted right now she was having a difficult time with any coherent thought other than "take your shirt off, cowboy."

He took a step closer, never looking away from her eyes, her mouth. "Your clothes are all wet again."

"They're your clothes," she countered.

The corner of his mouth tipped up. "Yours are dry now if you want to change."

She pulled in a deep breath, her breasts brushing against his chest. Had he closed the distance so tight or had she stepped forward? She'd been so mesmerized by his voice, his predatory gaze.

"Are you changing?" she asked.

Hayes reached behind his back and jerked the wet shirt up and over his head, tossing it onto the wood porch with a heavy smack. Ink covered his chest and up one shoulder. Dark hair glistened all over his pecs.

"You're not playing fair," she told him.

"Who said I was playing?"

He thrust his hands into her hair and covered her mouth before she could take a breath.

* * *

Taming the Texan
is part of Mills & Boon Desire's Nº1 bestselling series, Billionaires and Babies: Powerful men… wrapped around their babies' little fingers.

TAMING
THE TEXAN

BY
JULES BENNETT

All rights reserved including the right of reproduction in whole
or in part in any form. This edition is published by arrangement with
Harlequin Books S.A.

This is a work of fiction. Names, characters, places, locations and
incidents are purely fictional and bear no relationship to any real
life individuals, living or dead, or to any actual places, business
establishments, locations, events or incidents. Any resemblance is
entirely coincidental.

This book is sold subject to the condition that it shall not, by way of
trade or otherwise, be lent, resold, hired out or otherwise circulated
without the prior consent of the publisher in any form of binding or
cover other than that in which it is published and without a similar
condition including this condition being imposed on the subsequent
purchaser.

® and TM are trademarks owned and used by the trademark owner
and/or its licensee. Trademarks marked with ® are registered with the
United Kingdom Patent Office and/or the Office for Harmonisation in
the Internal Market and in other countries.

First Published in Great Britain 2017
By Mills & Boon, an imprint of HarperCollins*Publishers*
1 London Bridge Street, London, SE1 9GF

© 2017 Jules Bennett

ISBN: 978-0-263-07531-1

MIX
Paper from
responsible sources
FSC **FSC® C007454**
www.fsc.org

This book is produced from independently certified FSC™ paper
to ensure responsible forest management. For more information
visit www.harpercollins.co.uk/green.

Printed and bound in Great Britain
by CPI Group (UK) Ltd, Croydon, CR0 4YY

National bestselling author **Jules Bennett** has penned over forty contemporary romance novels. She lives in the Midwest with her high-school-sweetheart husband and their two kids. Jules can often be found on Twitter chatting with readers, and you can also connect with her via her website, julesbennett.com.

This book is for anyone who suffers from PTSD, depression, anxiety…please know you're not alone.

One

"What are you doing here, Ma'am?"

Alexa Rodriguez spun around, her hand to her heart. The low, gravelly voice had shocked her, but not as much as seeing the man strut toward her.

Well, he had a cowboy swagger with a slight limp, so she wouldn't quite call it a strut. Regardless of the label, the man held her attention and there was nowhere to go…not when she was pinned in place by that dark-as-night stare.

When she first stepped into the impressive stables on Pebblebrook Ranch, she hadn't seen a soul. And now this sexy cowboy stood only feet away, staring at her from beneath the wide brim of his black hat. Her heart shouldn't be beating so fast, so hard. But…yeah, he was one sexy stable hand.

Was she trespassing? The owner of the bed-and-breakfast next door had told Alexa the stables were open to B and B guests, but maybe there was some disconnect because this man did not look happy to have a visitor.

"I'm a guest next door," she explained as she tried to keep eye contact and not fidget. "I was told I could come ride and that someone would be here to assist me."

The stable hand grunted, but never took his eyes off her. Well, this was awkward.

Stepping out of her comfort zone was the theme of the weekend. Her meddling yet well-meaning best friend had bought Alexa a package for a three-night stay at the B and B, stating Alexa was an overworked single mom who deserved some alone time.

Alexa had just registered next door and put her bag in her room when she decided to check out the outdoor amenities before the predicted storm moved in. She hadn't been on a horse since she was five. Yeah, she was so far outside her comfort zone she didn't even know where comfort was anymore.

But if the horse came equipped with a captivating cowboy, maybe doing something different wouldn't be such a bad thing. Her best friend would definitely be thrilled Alexa was showing signs of life in the lust department, that was for sure.

This stable hand had sultry written all over him, from the dusty boots to the fitted denim over narrow hips to the black hat. And the way he drawled out the word *ma'am* had her stomach tingling.

Clearly, it had been too long since she'd had interaction with someone outside her preschool special education classroom and her fourteen-month-old son.

"You ever ridden before?" he finally asked.

"Once," she admitted, shoving her hands into the pockets of her jeans. "I was five and at a cousin's birthday party."

He took a step closer, minimizing the gap between them, and all the breath in Alexa's lungs seemed to vanish. How could one man be so striking, so bold? The deep eyes with long, dark lashes and a stubbled jaw outlining the most perfectly shaped lips…and that was all just his face.

Broad shoulders stretched his button-up black shirt in the most glorious way, one that had her imagining what excellent muscle tone he must have beneath the fabric. Those lean hips covered with well-worn denim could make any woman beg…but not her. She'd sworn off men who made her tingle—they were nothing but a hindrance in the life she'd carved out for her and her son.

And this man? He looked like pure trouble. The kind of trouble that could make a woman forget all common sense, the kind that would have a woman crying out his name over and over, the kind—

No. Her days of flirting or dating or anything else with a man were over—at least until her son got older and she could focus on her own life. For now, Mason was her everything and all that mattered.

Still, that didn't mean she couldn't look and appreciate…and there was so much to appreciate with this cowboy.

"Do you work here?" She had to assume so, but now she wondered if he was a guest, too.

He held out his hand. "Hayes Elliott."

Elliott. She wasn't just ogling any stable hand or random guest. Hayes was the elusive, mysterious war-veteran Elliott brother. Living in Stone River, she'd heard rumors about how he never left the ranch and the term PTSD had circulated nearly every time she'd heard his name.

Also what had cropped up along with his name was how he'd saved several children in a small village overseas and then been left severely injured, and how some of his friends had died in the same battle.

Something like that alone would make waves across a small town like Stone River, but couple the rumors with the fact that Hayes was a member of the prestigious Elliott family, well…it was difficult not to have gossip.

So where were his employees? A spread this large surely had several workers so the owners didn't have to lift a finger. She knew the Elliott brothers were gearing up to open a dude ranch on their five-thousand-acre spread. What she didn't know was why this brother, the sibling scarcely seen since he'd returned home, was the only one around.

"Alexa Rodriguez."

She gripped his hand and, though it was cliché, she felt… Well, she felt legitimate sparks. Sparks she hadn't experienced for years, and never at just the simple touch of a man's hand. How did that even happen?

"You're staying at my sister-in-law's bed-and-breakfast?" he asked, still holding on to her hand and looking her over.

Alexa nodded, impressed that he knew the goings-on of the B and B—but even more impressed at how her entire body responded to a handshake and a heavy-lidded stare. "I arrived this morning and thought I'd venture out before the storm."

And because she missed Mason. Alexa had already texted Sadie three times and requested a picture of him.

"My sister-in-law has the best B and B in Texas."

The low tone combined with a dimple that appeared when he spoke drew her attention to his mouth…a place she should not be looking. Granted, the rest of him was just as impressive. So where was a girl supposed to look when presented with such an intriguing man? Even his dusty boots were intriguing. They instantly sparked fantasies of him doing manual labor around the ranch... shirtless, to show off those sweaty, tanned muscles.

"The stable hands are all gone for the day. How long will you be staying next door?"

Well, that pulled her right from her glorious daydream.

"I'm here through the weekend," she replied, nerves swirling through her belly. "I, um... I didn't know they were gone, and I wanted to check things out before the weather turned. Sorry if I disturbed you."

The horse behind her stomped its foot as if protesting. She sort of felt like doing the same. She'd talked herself into taking a ride even though she wasn't completely comfortable, because she wanted to do something for herself and she didn't want to feel guilty about her friend paying for this getaway.

When Hayes continued to stare at her without a word, she got the impression he didn't want to be having this conversation any more than she did at this point. He obviously hadn't expected to find someone in his stable, especially when he thought his workers were gone.

The awkward silence had her offering a feeble smile before she turned. No need to stay where she obviously wasn't wanted.

"Wait." Hayes muttered a curse beneath his breath that had her cringing. "I'll take you out if you really want to go."

Alexa fisted her hands at her sides and pulled in a deep breath. Hayes's boots shuffled behind her as the horses shifted in their stalls. It was almost as if they were waiting for her answer.

"Listen." She turned, but stopped short when she realized he'd moved in closer than she expected. "I don't want to put you out."

There went that stare again, the one that held her in place and made her wonder what he was thinking… because the way he looked at her seemed an awful lot like— No, it couldn't be.

Why would someone like Hayes Elliott look at her with desire? He was a sexy cowboy, a war hero, a wealthy rancher and she was, well…just a single mom and schoolteacher.

"I came to take a ride now that everyone is gone," he explained. "Might as well take you."

Didn't that sound like a lovely invitation? All warm and sincere and wrapped in Southern hospitality.

"That's okay," she replied. "It's obvious you want to be alone."

She turned to go again, more than ready to get out of here. So far her vacation consisted of irritating a grouchy cowboy. The weekend could only get better from here…right?

"Damn it. Don't go."

Alexa laughed and spun back around. "It's fine. Really."

"No. I'm just not used to dealing with guests. It's supposed to rain later and over the next two days." He shrugged and shoved his hands in his pockets. "You're here now. Let's do this."

Let's get this over with.

The unspoken words hovered in the air between them. Fine. She wanted to ride and he was here. It wasn't her fault he was the only one left or that he was angry.

The sulking, sultry cowboy continued to stare at her

from beneath that Stetson and another jolt of lust shot through her.

Who knew a cranky rancher would be the one to get her heart beating again? She'd been pretty emotionally stagnant since becoming a widow two years ago, just before discovering she was pregnant. Grief and motherhood could do that.

"You'll ride Jumper."

Hayes's words pulled her to the present before she could dive too far into the dark time of her life. Alexa took a step back and held up her hands.

"Maybe you missed the part where I hadn't ridden since I was five. I think I'd rather have a horse with a name like Buttercup or Princess."

Hayes reached just past her, causing Alexa to freeze in place. His arm brushed against her shoulder and Alexa attempted to act calm. But that smell, that purely masculine aftershave, enveloped her. For a half second she breathed in deep and cursed herself for the instant carnal thoughts that flooded her mind.

"Jumper is our newest mare and she's a sweetheart," Hayes explained, oblivious to Alexa's inner turmoil. "We're getting her used to riding long distances and she'll be perfect for you. Don't be fooled by her name."

Alexa took a step to the side to get away from his casual touch. When she focused on the horse instead of the man, Alexa noticed a gorgeous chestnut mare with a white star on her nose.

"She's my favorite girl." He rubbed the side of her face and murmured something to her. "I got her specifically for new riders and children at the dude ranch because she's so gentle."

"You'll stick close?" she asked as she came to stand beside him. "I mean, I literally have no experience."

Hayes eyed her from beneath the large black rim of his hat. "No experience, huh?"

He raked that heavy-lidded gaze over her and he might as well have touched her bare skin. There wasn't a place on her that wasn't tingling. She'd met the man only five minutes ago and he'd managed to awaken something in her that had been dead for two years.

"You're in luck." He brought those dark eyes back up to hers. "I'm very…experienced."

Okay, they were definitely not talking horses anymore. There wasn't a doubt in her mind this man was much more worldly than she'd ever thought of being. If she had to guess, she'd put him in his midthirties, nearly a decade older than her own twenty-five.

"And I'll definitely stick close," he promised.

The ride hadn't even started and Alexa was already wondering if she was getting in over her head.

What the hell was he thinking?

He shouldn't be offering rides to or flirting with a total stranger. He'd come down to the stables to be alone, to ride his brother's stallion. Being back on the ranch was supposed to help him return to some semblance of the life he'd had before he'd been gutted by experiencing things no one should ever be subjected to.

But the second he'd hinted that she'd have to come back later for a stable hand to take her on a trail ride, a burst of jealousy speared him. The feeling had caught him off guard. He didn't want to feel, didn't want to allow himself any happiness. He'd been through hell and was just trying to survive each day and uphold his promise to his brothers and his ailing father. They had a dude ranch to get up and running and Hayes had a home to renovate.

Hayes had been back home a few months and he was not looking forward to getting involved with anyone right now...if ever. So no matter how mesmerizing Alexa's brown eyes were, no matter how she seemed to be a little sad and vulnerable, sparking that fierce protective instinct inside of him...he simply couldn't act on this unwanted chemistry.

He saw how she looked at him; he wasn't a fool. She was young; she was attracted. He was only going to show her a portion of the ranch, bring her back, and send her on her way. That would be the end of things. Her attraction had no place here...and neither did his.

He carried too much baggage, had too much to sort through within himself before he could think of trying anything with a woman again. Hell, he barely left the ranch, let alone attempted to be social and date.

Taking a beautiful woman out for a ride didn't have to be anything more than just that. Once she was gone, he could ride alone like he'd originally intended. Adjusting to civilian life was more difficult than he'd believed possible and riding alone was the only thing that cleared his mind.

PTSD was nothing to mess with, and he needed space. Perhaps a little one-on-one time with a total stranger wouldn't be such a bad thing. With Alexa, there would be no need for him to talk about himself. He didn't have to put on a front like he often did with his brothers. He could talk up the dude ranch with Alexa, which was a welcome distraction in his life. This family project might be the only thing keeping him from going out of his mind and giving in to the demons that had followed him home.

"I'll get her ready and we'll go," he told Alexa.

Alexa. Such a beautiful name for a woman with such

striking features. He'd only heard the name one other time, long ago. His high school buddy had dated and married someone named Alexa. Hayes had to force himself to stop staring because she was the type of woman a man could get lost in.

All that long midnight hair, her dark skin tone and those wide, chocolate eyes. Her curves were damn near hypnotic in those jeans and fitted tank. Yeah, she would turn any man's head and he was no exception.

Years of military training had enabled him to mask his emotions—something that would come in handy on a trail ride with this beauty. The sooner he could get this ride over with, the better.

Hayes saddled up Jumper and Doc, his brother's stallion. Nolan had been working overtime at the hospital, so Hayes had offered to get Nolan's horse out for exercise.

"Right this way, Ma'am."

If he didn't refer to her by her name, maybe he could keep this little escapade impersonal…exactly the way he wanted to live his life. Detached.

Hayes took the reins and led the horses from the stable. Alexa fell in step beside him. The subtle aroma of jasmine tickled his senses. His instincts hadn't failed him in all his years overseas, and he was positive he had Alexa pegged as someone who wasn't taking time away because she necessarily wanted to. Something about her reserved nature and an underlying hint of fear made him all the more determined to make this ride to be enjoyable and memorable for her.

After all, wasn't Pebblebrook using Annabelle's B and B as a way to spread the word for the dude ranch? By the time they were ready to open, they would not only have her guests already talking, they'd also have hired the best PR firm in the country. This dude ranch was a goal of their father's and Hayes wasn't about to let that man down.

"You live on the ranch?" she asked as they stepped out into the bright June sunshine.

"I do." That was the easy answer. The ranch was now in its third generation of Elliotts, and Hayes wouldn't want to be anywhere else. He owned two other homes: one in the mountains of Montana and a tropical getaway in the secluded part of the main island of Hawaii. He had options, but the ranch was where he'd come to heal, to find that piece of himself that had been damaged... possibly destroyed for good.

"There are several homes on the ranch," he continued. "My brother Colt and his wife, Annabelle, live in the first house you see as you come up the drive. Nolan and his wife live in the back on the east side, and I live in the original Elliott homestead back on the west corner. It's set between the river and the brook running through the ranch."

He loved not only owning that piece of history from his family, but having the privacy he so desperately craved right now. His brothers respected the fact that he needed his space.

"Sounds like quite a family," she stated. She wrung her hands as she glanced back to Jumper. "Are you sure the horse is safe for me? Does she know I'm nervous?"

Hayes looped Doc's reins around the post and moved to Jumper's side, right by Alexa. "You're not nervous. You're anxious. There's a difference."

Alexa smiled, a simple gesture that packed a punch of lust straight to his gut. Damn it, he didn't want a punch of any kind. Couldn't he just enjoy the company of a beautiful woman without lust entering into the picture? He wanted this ride to be simple, but the stirring in his body was anything but.

Someone should've notified Annabelle not to send any guests up today because the stable hands had all gone with Colt to the auction for more steers, leaving Hayes in charge. Not a position he'd wanted to be in.

Despite all the pain and anguish and betrayal he'd been through, something about Alexa made him want to get closer. Perhaps it was all those curves packed into such a petite frame, maybe it was those striking eyes that seemed to look deeper than just the surface, or perhaps it was that underlying vulnerability that made his inner protector surge to the forefront. Regardless, he knew this ride wasn't going to be quick and painless like he'd first intended.

"At any time, we can turn back," he stated, hoping that would give him the out he desperately wanted.

Alexa nodded. "I'm ready. Just tell me what to do so I don't hurt or scare her."

"Grab the pommel and hook your left foot into the stirrup."

She followed his command and, before he even realized what he was doing, he'd stepped in behind her and circled her waist with his hands. Alexa stilled beneath his touch. Throwing a glance over her shoulder, her eyes met his.

"I'm helping you up." He left no room for argument because, while he might not have thought about his actions at first, now that he had his hands on her, he was in no hurry to let go. "Relax," he murmured.

Her eyes darted to his mouth—as if he needed another reason to feel that pull of sexual tension. Those dark lashes framed striking eyes and all of that rich black hair slid over her shoulders, the tips brushing against the backs of his hands. An image of all of that hair sliding over his body came to mind and Hayes knew in that instant he was fighting a losing battle.

He wanted this woman, the first woman he'd wanted since his return. And he planned to have her... To hell with all the reasons this ride was a bad idea. He'd just figured out the reason this was the best idea he'd had in months.

Two

This was not a good idea. Nope, nope, nope. As if the horse agreed with her, each nope in her mind fell in tandem with each stomp of a hoof.

Alexa wished she could just ignore the zing shooting through her, but how could she? This man was the first to strike any type of spark or interest in so long… There was no ignoring the emotions.

She'd done well to mask her feelings for years, but there was no way she could lie to herself right now. Hayes Elliott was one sexy cowboy, and he had the brooding, broad-shoulder thing down to perfection. And those jeans? Yeah, they fit gloriously over lean hips that produced the sexiest swagger she'd ever seen. Even with the minor limp, Hayes was intriguing and every part of her wanted to know more.

Down, girl. Alexa hadn't come on this little getaway to find some cowboy. Though Hayes Elliott would no doubt fuel her fantasies for a good long time.

Alexa's horse stayed alongside his. Clearly, this wasn't the first time they'd been out together. Her hips rocked back and forth in the saddle with the motion of Jumper's easy gait. Alexa didn't even want to glance over to see what Hayes's hips were doing. Her eyes needed to stay straight ahead.

The picturesque ranch was breathtaking. White fencing ran as far as the eye could see. The rolling hills were dotted with cattle in the distance. With the bright sun beating down on the land, Alexa found it hard to believe a storm would be rolling in soon.

She wanted to focus on enjoying the ride, but on occasion Hayes's thigh would brush against hers and those tingles would start up all over again.

Good grief. She'd met the man only moments ago and already he held such power over her... How was that even possible?

Maybe she'd been too enveloped in her classroom and her son. Alexa needed to venture out more, as Sadie had said when she'd insisted Alexa take this vacation, but in her normal life...well, where would she go? It wasn't as if she had guys asking her out or a large group of friends she went out with. She had Sadie, who taught in the class next to hers. They'd met in college and had been friends since. And she had Mason.

Alexa was fine being a single mother with not much of a social life. Her job right now was to be both mother and father to Mason, so anything else would have to wait. And that was more than okay. She had one guy in her life and he was more than enough.

"How long has this land been in your family?" she asked, desperate for a topic that would get her mind off the rugged, moody man and slice through the tension between them.

"My brothers and I are third-generation ranchers at Pebblebrook. My grandfather built the house that I live in."

So he had mentioned before. "How many acres are there?"

"Over five thousand."

Alexa had read that in the pamphlet for the B and B, which advertised the upcoming dude ranch. She'd asked because the last thing she wanted was silence. That would only be awkward and cause her daydreaming to start all over again.

Alexa couldn't even imagine trying to keep up with all this land and the livestock, but of course the Elliotts had the funds to hire people to do all the maintenance and grunt work.

Her world consisted of wrangling four-year-olds all day and coming home to a rambunctious baby boy. Her life was quite different from the Elliotts' ranch lifestyle. Part of her was proud of herself for taking this break Sadie had insisted and paid for. The other part of her wondered if Mason had enjoyed his morning snack of blueberries and bananas.

Maybe she should stop to call and check in.

"That's the first barn my grandfather built on this land."

Hayes cut into her thoughts with the history of the ranch. Up ahead, Alexa spotted a small barn, definitely old in comparison to the massive stone-and-metal structure at the beginning of the property. The Elliotts might be billionaires, but she could see the way they'd grown this estate from something small into something grand.

"You doin' all right?" Even with the concerned question, Hayes had that low, gruff tone.

"Fine," she replied.

"Want to explore more?"

Or turn back.

Alexa wasn't quite ready to head back, but at the same time she knew he didn't want to be out here with her. He probably preferred privacy.

"I could stay out here forever," she replied, finding it to be true. "But I don't want to keep you."

He grunted, whatever that meant.

"Was that a reply?" she asked as she glanced over to him. It was nearly impossible to see his face in the shadow from his hat's wide brim.

"I've got nothing," he replied, sounding way too lost, too broken.

Alexa glanced at his hands on the reins. Scars randomly crossed over his taut knuckles. Those large, tanned hands no doubt had done so much. He was a soldier, a rancher. Everything about him screamed alpha and loner. For some insane reason, she found that attractive. She chalked it up to the fact that she always looked out for those in need, not that she found him irresistibly sexy.

Hayes was the exact opposite of her late husband. Before Scott had passed away, they'd been so in love and ready to spend the rest of their lives together. He was safe, made her *feel* safe. She hadn't felt that way since he'd died of heart disease. The doctors had tried to comfort her by telling her there was no way they could have known he'd been born with the defect that had ultimately taken his life.

She hadn't been able to save him. Not that she was a medical professional, but she had survivor's guilt. There was no way to dodge it. And finding out she was pregnant only a week after she'd lost him had only added to the guilt.

Alexa was familiar with the emotion, even before Scott died. She had been only eight when her sister drowned while they were swimming. On their family vacation to the beach, they'd both gone out too far. A riptide pulled her sister out and it was all her father could do to save Alexa from being swept under as well. Years of remorse and counseling had held her family together.

So Alexa recognized the brokenness Hayes displayed.

Alexa gripped her reins and enjoyed the steady trot. They were going a bit faster than before and she figured Hayes had urged his horse to speed up and hers had followed suit. Someone like Hayes wouldn't ask permission first, but he kept glancing her way to check on her.

"So you're the only one around today?" she asked, needing to break up the thoughts swirling around in her head about the sexy man brushing his thigh against hers.

"There are a few workers milling about," he replied. "I just happened to be the only one in the stables."

"But you weren't working."

He threw her a glance and adjusted his hat. "I'd just gotten done at my house and decided to take a break and ride."

So he *had* been planning on going out alone. "You could've told me to come back later."

"I could've, but as you said, there's a storm coming in later. You would've thought I was a jerk."

Alexa couldn't help but laugh. "You wouldn't have felt bad for sending me away?"

Hayes shrugged and turned his horse slightly. Alexa followed. "I don't have feelings anymore, but this is my family's ranch and I know how hard they've worked."

"So it's about respect, then." When he remained silent, she went on. "Whatever it is, I apologize for taking you away from your personal time and I appreciate you showing me the grounds."

As they continued toward the back of the property, the sky darkened slightly and thick clouds rolled in. Texas weather was crazy; pop up showers and storms were the norm. She didn't think it was supposed to do much until later this afternoon.

If it was stormy over the next few days, as predicted, she could lounge in that oversize garden tub in her suite back at the B and B. The moment she'd stepped foot in the house she could tell no expense had been spared. The beauty of the house and her bathroom—hello, heated floors—made her want to move in and bring Mason with her.

The first fat raindrop landed on her nose. Then, before they could find shelter, the skies opened up and Hayes cursed. The next thing she knew, he'd plunked his cowboy hat on top of her head. The gesture shouldn't have touched her, but beneath his gruff exterior and grunting dialogue, he had a big heart. The fact that he was a true gentleman warmed something deep inside her, something that hadn't warmed in quite a while.

"Storm came sooner than I thought," he called over the sound of the pouring rain. "Follow me."

He and Doc took the lead and started trotting faster. Alexa gripped her reins tighter and kept up, her bottom bouncing in the saddle as the rain continued to soak through her clothes. She wasn't comfortable with the faster speed, but all she could do was hold on for the ride and pray they weren't going far.

They rode another few minutes and Alexa was starting to wonder where they were heading. Then, up ahead, she saw an old two-story farmhouse. Hayes's house. She didn't have to ask—she knew. It was just as she'd imagined an old farmhouse should look.

The white home with black shutters had a first and second-story porch and a pitched gable right in the center of the roofline. So adorable, and much different from the grand home his brother lived in on the other side of the property. This house seemed simpler, tucked in the back of the ranch as if protected.

Is that why Hayes chose to live here? So he could be away from everything and remain safe? The man might scream badass, but even after their short acquaintance she could tell he was on guard at all times. Just how deep did his pain run?

Beneath the brim of the borrowed hat, Alexa took in the beauty of the house…even through the raindrops. The brook ran alongside the home and the river flowed behind it. The house and a barn were nestled up on the hilly part of the land.

Hayes rode straight to the small barn at the side of the house. As the showers continued to pummel them, she followed and before she could hop down, he was at her side. His hand landed on her thigh, doing nothing to help with those tremors she'd been experiencing since meeting Mr. Elliott.

That hand slid up to her waist as she swung one leg over and dismounted. The brim of the hat bumped against him and fell off her head to land at her feet. His hands remained on her hips to steady her and Alexa gripped his biceps…and those muscles were just as impressive as she'd thought they'd be.

His eyes darted to her lips and Alexa didn't care about the rain anymore. She didn't care if snowflakes started falling from the sky or a tornado ripped through.

She wanted to stay just like this—it wasn't like she could get any more soaked—and have Hayes look at her like he desired her.

Oh, this was lust at its finest, but it had been so long since anyone had looked at her lips, she didn't care. Lust was a welcome emotion at this point. After two years of nothing, the idea that someone might find her attractive was quite the turn-on. The defined, taut body beneath her fingertips didn't hurt, either.

The muscle clenched in his jaw beneath that dark stubble. "Get up on the porch."

The angry tone left her wondering just what, or who, he was upset with. The fact they got caught in the rain or the fact that he clearly wanted to kiss her and opted to have restraint?

"Tell me what to do." She reached for the horse's reins. "In the barn?"

He shook his head and swiped his hat off the ground before striding back to his horse. Hayes led them into the barn and secured each horse in their own stall.

"Hopefully the rain will pass soon." He didn't even look at her as he closed the stall doors. "The bigger storm wasn't forecast until much later. You can wait here or go onto the porch."

A rumble of thunder had her wondering just how quickly this would pass.

Hayes jerked his gaze toward the opening of the stable at the storm's approach. She hadn't taken him for someone who was afraid of storms. Pop-ups weren't uncommon in Stone River, but since it was supposed to rain all weekend, she wondered if the storm had already begun. They might just have to ride back in the rain.

"We can go back," she told him. "I mean, it's not like

I'm going to get any wetter. Or I can ride back alone.
I know the way."

Hayes turned to focus on her now, and man did those
dark eyes focus. He raked his gaze over her like he was
one leap away from pouncing. Alexa's skin heated just
the same as if he'd touched her with his hands.

Mercy sakes, she'd known the man maybe an hour.
Clearly, she needed to get out more if the first good-
looking rancher made her want to sit up and beg.

"When you go back, you won't be going alone," he
told her. "We'll wait. It's a downpour and a long ride
back."

The showers beat down on the old metal roof and
there was something calming, refreshing about being
out here without a care in the—

"Oh no." Alexa cringed. "My cell phone."

She patted the pocket where she'd stored it, but her
pants were wet. She only hoped her cell had survived.
She couldn't be cut off from contact with her son. This
was her first trip away. She needed to cling to texts
and video chats.

"Texts to your boyfriend can wait."

Alexa squared her shoulders and swiped her damp
hair away from her face. "That wasn't subtle, if you
were asking if I was single."

"I wasn't asking."

Yet that gaze never wavered from hers and those
heavy lids said otherwise. Hayes might not want to be
attracted to her, but he was and he was none too happy
about it.

"Sure you were," she countered. "You keep looking at my mouth and wondering what it would be like
to kiss me, so don't pretend you didn't want to know
if I'm taken."

There went the old Alexa again. Scott had always told her she was bold. She'd always said what was on her mind, because…why play games? But since his death, she'd been quieter, more reserved.

Apparently the moody cowboy brought out the best in her.

"You're an attractive woman," he replied. It shocked her that he was just as blunt. "I'm a guy. But don't worry, sweetheart. Your lips are safe from mine."

Cocky *cabron*. Like she'd asked for a kiss?

Alexa spun away and jogged through the rain to the safety of the back porch. The old swing swayed in the wind as another rumble of thunder rolled through. She crossed the porch and took a seat. Pulling her hair over her shoulder, she squeezed out the excess water.

Glancing back to the barn, Alexa saw Hayes standing in the opening, hands on his hips, black hair plastered to his head from the rain. He stared across the yard at her as if trying to decipher his next move.

Well, he could think all he wanted, but she was staying right here until it was time to roll out…or whatever lingo ranchers used. Wagons ho?

As if she didn't have a care in the world, Alexa used the toe of her boot to push off the concrete. Even though she was completely soaked through, she sat on Hayes's porch swaying back and forth as if this were a sunny summer day and she was sipping a cold glass of Southern sweet tea. As if this were her own home… If she really stretched her imagination, she could picture Mason toddling around in the grass, splashing in the puddles.

Wait. She needn't get swept away in her own dreams. Fantasizing about a sexy cowboy was one thing, but imagining herself here with her son was flat-out dangerous.

Just because she'd been saving for a home of her own with a yard for Mason didn't mean she should picture him here. This was Elliott property. This was *Hayes*'s property. To be here with Mason would mean an emotional investment she wasn't ready to make.

Hayes started across the yard, favoring his left side, walking as casually as you please, as if he weren't getting pelted by rain. Oh, that control he managed to cling to was so maddening, even more so because she didn't seem to have any of her own at the moment.

The entire time he closed the distance between them, he had those dark eyes fixed on her.

Alexa swallowed and attempted to give herself a mental pep talk on not getting tangled up with this frustrating, captivating cowboy. But the closer he got, the more her nerves danced around in her belly.

She had a feeling her interesting day had just gotten started.

Three

Being drenched did absolutely nothing to get his mind back on track. Granted, his life in general hadn't been in the right place since he'd signed up for the Army at eighteen.

How the hell had this simple trail ride turned into Miss Alexa, of the swinging hips and sultry midnight eyes, nestled on his porch swing? Since when did he ever let anyone else take control of his life?

Oh, yeah. Ever since his former fiancée betrayed him with their commanding officer while he was fighting for his country, seeing things no man or woman should ever have to see. Clearly, he hadn't had control over that situation.

Hayes stepped up onto the porch and leaned against the post. "You might as well come inside," he told her. "This doesn't look like it will pass anytime soon, after all."

She braced her feet to stop the swaying swing. "I'm

soaking wet. I don't need to go in. I'm quite happy swinging and watching the storm. With those dark clouds, I bet it will be a doozy."

Hayes sighed. "Don't be ridiculous. You're drenched and I can at least offer dry clothes and put yours in the dryer."

"Oh, don't be so cliché," she told him as she came to her feet. "Wearing your clothes during a storm? Next, you'll find some way that we need to share body heat by wearing nothing."

Hayes had actually thought of that, but he wasn't about to mention it now. She clearly had a low opinion of his intentions.

He forced himself not to stare at the way her jeans and her tank molded to every single dip and flare of her curves. A gorgeous woman with a killer body...it was like fate was seriously testing him. He wasn't in the mood to be tempted and he sure as hell wasn't in the mood for games.

"I'm going inside to change, you can come or you can stay out here and be wet. I don't give a damn." He crossed to the screen door and jerked on the handle. "And offering you clothes in a storm isn't cliché. It's called manners."

He stepped inside and eased the squeaking screen door shut without slamming it. The old linoleum in the entry hadn't been replaced in decades, so he wasn't too concerned about dripping in here.

Hayes headed toward the utility room off the kitchen. There was laundry in there he needed to put away, so he knew he'd find something for himself and he could throw his things in the dryer.

The loud bang behind him had Hayes crouched down in an instant, his hands coming up to shield his head.

But within two seconds he realized he was home, not in battle, and the slam came from the back door.

Slowly rising to his feet, he glanced over his shoulder to find Alexa staring down at him, her eyes wide with worry.

Damn it. He didn't want pity or empathy. Hell, he didn't want company, but that wasn't an option right now. Couldn't he ever fight these demons alone without witnesses? His brothers knew to keep their distance, and he'd come out of his house when he was having a good day…which happened to be earlier today, but now he was ready for privacy.

His heart still beat rapidly in his chest, he continued to stare at Alexa, silently daring her to apologize.

"I—I didn't know that would trigger something," she murmured. "What can I do?"

Clenching his fists at his sides, he willed his mind to chill out and stay focused on the fact that he was safe here on Pebblebrook.

Well, as safe as he could be with a soaking wet woman standing in his kitchen. She'd asked what she could do. That in and of itself was rather amazing.

He was so tired of everyone asking if he was okay. Hell no, he wasn't okay. Jumping at a door was not normal. Flipping out at the roll of thunder was damn embarrassing. He never knew what would set him off until it happened, so there was no way to prepare.

Well, except the screen door. He'd let it go once and it had slammed at his back and he'd flattened himself on the floor for several minutes before he came back to reality. He'd only made that mistake once, but he hadn't thought it would be an issue again because it wasn't like he had regular visitors.

"You want a change of clothes or not?" Hayes asked, ignoring her question.

He tugged at the hem of his soaked shirt and peeled it up and over his head. Clutching the wet material in his hand, he turned his attention back to Alexa.

Her eyes were fixed on his chest, no doubt zeroing in on the scars. Definitely not a story he wanted to get in to, but he wasn't ashamed of fighting for his country. He was only ashamed he'd been fool enough not to see the betrayal going on behind his back. But even that pain paled in comparison to the horrific scene in that tiny village where he'd been able to save the women and children, but not his brothers-in-arms.

"If you have a spare shirt, that would be great," she finally told him.

"What about your jeans?" He knew his were irritating him already.

"I don't wear your size."

Her instant sarcasm had him almost ready to crack a smile. Snarky comments were a staple in the lives of the Elliott brothers, so it was nice to talk to someone who wasn't coddling him. She'd asked what she could do to help, and not pushing the issue was going a long way.

"I'm a foot taller than you," he agreed. "But I'm sure I have sweats that you could fold up while you're waiting on your jeans to dry. Your call."

She propped her hands on her hips and tilted her head. "Do I get privacy or are we both changing in the middle of your kitchen?"

"Are you always so blunt?"

She shrugged, dropping her hands to her sides. "You bring out my sunny side."

Hayes shook his head and moved into the laundry room. He quickly found a gray T-shirt and a pair of navy sweatpants. Clutching the clothes, he came back into the kitchen.

"There's a half bath right through there," he said, pointing to the hallway that led to the front of the house. "You can change and bring me your wet things after."

As she stepped forward and closed the space between them, he couldn't ignore the stir of arousal. Why? Really, why did he have to be attracted to someone? One would think after what he'd been through he would be immune to women, but apparently that was not the case.

Maybe it was that initial vulnerability he'd seen in her at the stables. Perhaps it was all of that silken raven hair. Or maybe it was how she was clearly a strong woman who wasn't afraid to speak her mind.

Regardless, the sooner this storm passed, the sooner he could get her back where she belonged. Between his jumpiness and the unwanted attraction, this was going to be a hell of a storm...both inside and out.

The bathroom was just as dated and neglected as the kitchen. Which was rather surprising, considering the Elliotts had more money than she'd ever see in a lifetime.

But finances were the least of her concerns right now. For one thing, the shirt smelled amazing. So amazing, in fact, that she might have taken her time in sliding it down over her face so she could inhale that woodsy, masculine scent.

Her other concern was really the reason she hadn't stepped from the bathroom just yet. Where was she supposed to put her bra? It was soaked, so she wasn't going to keep it on. But it wasn't like she wanted to walk out and hand him her pink lacy demi. She'd only met the man a few hours ago. Him handling her unmentionables seemed a bit too intimate.

Grabbing her wet jeans, socks and tank, she wrapped the bra inside the wad of clothes and stepped barefoot from the bathroom.

Thankfully, her phone was okay. No messages from Sadie, so Alexa would check in later. She'd only been gone a few hours, so checking in now would seem over-bearing…though she probably would've already done so had this little predicament with Hayes not presented itself.

Hayes stood in the kitchen with his back to her, the coffeepot in the corner brewing to life. The sight of that broad back had her clutching her wet clothes and will-ing herself to calm down. He was just a man. A really sexy, intriguing, frustrating man who'd stared at her lips and stripped his shirt off in front of her.

"Can I throw these in?" she asked.

He glanced over his shoulder, his eyes flared slightly when he raked his gaze over her body. Yeah, his 2X shirt was nearly to her knees. Apparently he needed this size to accommodate those muscles, but she was neither muscular nor tall, so she looked utterly ridiculous. But she was dry and that's what mattered.

"I'll take them."

When he started toward her, she shook her head. "I can do it."

"Have a seat and give me the clothes. I've seen wom-en's underwear before."

Of course he'd know why she was clutching her things like a lifeline. "Well, you haven't seen mine."

Not a smile or a comment from him as he took her things and disappeared into the utility room. Alexa crossed to the coffeepot and nearly groaned at the glorious smell. She glanced at the bag on the counter and didn't recognize the brand. Probably something she couldn't just pick up in the corner market. The Elliotts probably had minions to handpick their coffee beans and make a special roast just for them.

She glanced around, surprised she'd missed the French press on the counter. This kitchen had an expensive coffee maker and a French press? Well, he apparently had his priorities in order.

"They should be done in about forty minutes," he told her as he came back in.

"The rain hasn't let up," she commented as she stared out the large window over the sink. "The sky is getting darker, too."

Not a good sign. Not good at all.

"I drove my truck down to the stables before riding the horses here with you and most everyone else on the ranch is gone for the day," he muttered, as if wondering how the hell to get her back to the other side of the property in the middle of this storm.

A bolt of lightning flashed through the sky. Now she was being mocked by Mother Nature. Apparently there was no good way to get back to a vehicle that could take her to the B and B.

Alexa wrapped her arms around her waist and glanced around the room. This was all so…awkward for her. She had a small town house in Stone River and lived with an infant. But here she was thrust into the country, into an old family home with a sexy man and wearing his clothes, which smelled far too fabulous. Part of her couldn't help but think back to another man and another T-shirt she used to wear.

But that was a lifetime ago and she was in a whole new world. Everything here was so foreign, yet so familiar. From the masculine scent to the intimacy of the moment to the rush of adrenaline when Hayes had been staring at her lips out in the rain.

"You're not afraid of storms are you?"

Hayes's question pulled her from her thoughts. The way he studied her from across the room had her wondering if he always stared with such intensity.

"No, no."

Silence settled heavy between them and Alexa didn't know how to keep this situation from getting more uncomfortable.

Smoothing her damp hair away from her face, Alexa met Hayes's steady stare. "Don't let me get in your way," she told him. "I can sit here and drink coffee and you can do…whatever it is that you do."

He continued to stare, not showing an ounce of emotion. "I don't do much other than renovate this place when I'm not working on the ranch."

He worked? Like, manual labor? Alexa knew the Elliotts were well-known ranchers, but she figured they handled the glamorous side of things and hired out all the work.

"Well, point me toward the coffee mugs and I can take it from there. I'll just wait for the storm to pass."

Hayes stared another minute, then turned to the cabinet to pull her down a navy mug. He set it on the counter and walked out of the room.

Alexa simply stood there, staring at the now empty hallway. Apparently Hayes wasn't in the hosting mood. Oh well, she'd told him to go about his business and clearly that's what he intended to do.

Fine by her. She didn't want to annoy him any more than she apparently already had.

Four

Hayes flattened his palms on his desk and blew out a sigh. What the hell was he doing?

Not that he had much choice in what to do next with his unexpected guest. He might want to be left alone to battle his demons and renovate his home, but he couldn't be a jerk. That's not how he'd been raised. The Elliott boys had been taught how to treat people, and women were always treated with the utmost respect. His father had handled his marriage as if Hayes's mother was royalty.

Which was why Hayes had had to walk out of the kitchen. Because Alexa standing there in his clothes was too damn tempting. He respected her, even though she was driving him insane. Walking away was his only option.

While he wouldn't mind a little stress reliever in the most primal, old-fashioned way, something about her screamed innocence and vulnerability. He could find a better use for that sassy mouth of hers, but yet again, that desire waved every red flag inside his mind.

Yes, he wanted the hell out of her, but that was just lust. Alexa didn't seem like the type to give in to lustful feelings.

Unless properly persuaded.

He deliberately turned his thoughts to the storm. The rain pounded against the windows and the thunder continued to roll every few minutes. Thankfully, it wasn't booming. An occasional streak of lightning flashed across the sky. No, this storm wasn't letting up anytime soon. He'd thought for sure it wasn't going to do anything until tomorrow.

His eyes landed on the piece of mail he'd attempted to ignore. The governor had chosen the wrong recipient for the Man of Honor award.

This was a new award and apparently Hayes had been the first choice. When they'd called him last week to inform him, he'd been numb, shocked, then angry. Hayes didn't want a damn award for serving his country. He didn't want to be recognized because he'd been the only one in his platoon to survive. His busted-up knee was nothing compared to what his brothers had gone through.

Pushing away from his desk, he turned and headed out of his office and down the hall to the kitchen. The last thing he wanted was to see that damn gold-embossed invitation.

Initially, he'd thought working in his office would allow him to ignore Alexa. He figured he'd look over some of the dude ranch plans, but then the invitation mocked him. And now he felt guilty for walking out on her without saying a word.

His brothers, Nolan and Colt, were moving forward

with the transformation of a portion of the ranch property. It wouldn't be long before Pebblebrook's dude ranch would be up and running and pulling in tourists just like their father had always wanted. Even though he was in a nursing facility and not in his right mind, his sons planned to push through and keep the patriarch informed each step of the way. He might not recall his plans, but the boys needed the communication with their dad.

Well, three of the four boys. Colt's twin, Beau, wasn't part of the process. He was too busy out in LA, making movies and being Hollywood's playboy to worry with the ranch. Or at least that's the way it seemed. The media loved any scoop they could get on the so-called "it" actor and, as of late, Beau had been seen in some compromising pictures with an up-and-coming actress.

Beau would occasionally call or text one of his brothers, but more often than not, he couldn't be reached because he was off in some remote location working... and whatever else he did.

Hayes kept his true feelings for Beau's choices to himself. He and Beau didn't mesh well on a good day, so it was probably best Colt's twin wasn't around. It was crazy how Colt and Beau were identical twins, but Colt worked his ass off at the ranch while Beau would rather smile pretty for the camera. Definitely night-and-day brothers.

Hayes entered the kitchen and came up short. Alexa had the back door propped open while she examined the screen door. She muttered under her breath and Hayes couldn't make out quite what she was saying, but she seemed extremely determined in whatever it was she was doing.

Intrigued about what she was attempting, Hayes

crossed his arms and leaned against the door frame leading from the hall to the kitchen. Alexa opened the screen wider, then eased it back. She fiddled with the spring at the top and slid the stopper along the bar in the middle. Then she eased the door back and forth again.

Hayes chewed on the inside of his lip and tried not to focus on how slender her shoulders were beneath his T-shirt, or how she'd had to fold the waistband and the cuffs of the pants just so they'd somewhat fit. The stirring of normal emotions felt so foreign, he was starting to wonder if she'd put a spell on him. How could one voluptuous woman with eyes dark as night be so enthralling?

Her long black hair had started to dry and hung in ropelike waves down her back. He clenched his fists against his chest and ignored the fantasy of how silky all that hair would feel sliding between his fingertips… because he'd never know. Letting his mind wander was a moot point.

Alexa shifted slightly and met his eyes. Her hands stilled on the door as she slowly brought it to a close. The pounding rain blew in on his back porch and the porch swing tapped a rhythm against the side of the house.

"Sorry. I just… I thought maybe I could fix the door and keep it from slamming so hard."

Even though her eyes never wavered from his, the rest of her body language showed she was completely nervous. She wrapped her arms around her waist, pulling the material tighter and showcasing the fact that she wore nothing beneath his shirt.

His body betrayed him and stirred with arousal.

"Do you often go around fixing stranger's doors?"

She tipped her head and offered a slight grin. "I'm

wearing your clothes, so I'm not sure how much of a stranger you are. Besides, I fixed my own door at home, so I thought I could work on yours."

He could fix the damn thing himself, but he'd just gotten used to closing it softly, and not fixing it was more about the principle now. He wasn't about to let that door win. It was a damn door and he refused to be intimidated by it.

Besides, it wasn't like anyone ever stopped by. Occasionally his brothers would drop in, but usually they were in the old barn or Hayes saw them down at the main stables. With his house tucked away on the farthest corner of the property, there wasn't much use for anyone to come back here. All the livestock were kept on the west side more toward Nolan's home.

"Are you that bored?" he asked.

She stepped further into the kitchen, shutting the oak door at her back and drowning out the sound of the rain pelting the back porch. "I didn't want to get in your way. When you left a while ago, it seemed like you were angry that I was here."

Angry? No. Frustrated, sexually charged and confused as hell? Absolutely.

"I'm not angry with you."

He needed her to know that. It wasn't her fault she was stuck here with a guy who couldn't handle a door closing and who had the social skills of a wooden spoon.

Hayes remained in the doorway as she crossed the room. The way those curves moved beneath his clothes was so ridiculously hot. He hadn't been with a woman since his ex, but he hadn't been looking, either.

Yet here Alexa stood, all barefoot in his kitchen with her black hair down and those dark eyes showing way too much.

The woman couldn't hide her emotions and she wavered from vulnerable to turned on to unsure. And damn if all of those crystal clear emotions didn't make him want to pick her up and drag her to his room. He wanted to protect her, to figure out why she went from sassy to insecure in the span of seconds, and he wanted to kiss the hell out of those unpainted lips.

Damn her for calling him on that earlier. She'd pegged him…which only made him want her all the more.

"What are your plans for the kitchen?" she asked, stopping just in front of him.

Her random question threw him off. "My plans?"

"You said you're renovating," she reminded him. "And someone with that coffee setup surely has a grand idea of what he wants done in here."

Hayes pushed off the door and eased around her. How pathetic to be running from a curvaceous woman who was utterly harmless. Well, she wasn't exactly harmless or he wouldn't be so anxious. She made him achy and needy and he sure as hell did not like this unfamiliar emotional place he was in. Not one bit.

Hayes went to the coffee station he'd temporarily set up and poured himself a steaming mug. "I have plenty of plans, but everything takes time."

"What have you done so far in the rest of the house?" she asked as she turned to face him.

"Master bedroom and bath."

He was pretty proud of how the work had turned out. He'd done everything himself, often at night when he couldn't sleep.

"What are you working on next?" she asked.

Hayes shrugged. "You planning on pitching in?"

A ghost of a smile danced around her lips. "If that

rain doesn't let up, it could be a long night. Might as well find something to occupy our time."

The words were completely true, but now that she said them and they were hovering in the air between them, Hayes was having a hard time remembering why he was keeping his hands to himself.

If Alexa ended up being an overnight guest, he better find a project real soon to get started on or he'd have those clothes stripped off her before midnight.

"I plan on doing every room and then starting on the outside," he told her. "I have no timeline."

It wasn't like he was going anywhere. He'd come back to heal, in his own time, and to assist with the dude ranch. Renovating was simply a much needed distraction.

He'd had surgery on his leg in Germany before he came back to the States. Since then he'd done some in-home therapy, but he was stuck with this damn limp, a physical reminder of that horrendous day. So that portion of his healing had gone as far as possible. He wasn't too sure if the mental healing would make any better progress.

"You're doing all the work yourself?" she asked, tipping her head to the side.

"Why would I hire for it when I'm perfectly capable?"

Alexa shrugged and crossed to the kitchen table. She took a seat and rested her elbows on the scarred wooden top. "Because you're loaded."

Hayes stared for another minute before he let out a bark of laughter. He didn't remember the last time he'd actually laughed, but his temporary roommate was seriously getting through the wall he'd been hiding behind.

Maybe that was most of her appeal. She clearly knew

about the PTSD, she hadn't offered apologies and she didn't back down from what she wanted to say. All of that added up to one sexy package.

"There goes that honest mouth again."

One dainty fingertip traced a scarred pattern over the tabletop. "I mean, I love manual labor, but most people would rather just have someone else do the grunt work. Especially when they could afford to just tear this place down and build from scratch and make it five times the size."

He met her gaze. "I'm not like anyone you've ever met."

Dark eyes widened at his declaration. The whisky color called to him, but he knew that was just hormones talking. The electricity flickered, pulling him from the trance.

"Are you kidding me?" she muttered beneath her breath, her eyes rolling up to the ceiling.

"Eager to leave?"

Her eyes snapped back to his. "Aren't you just as eager to see me go?"

There were two ways he could answer that and both of them were honest. Yes, he wanted her to go because he hated visitors.

On the other hand, no. He wanted her to stay so he could watch her body move beneath his clothes a little longer. Masochism clearly had settled in deep here because at this point he'd rather be tormented by her snarky comments and her tempting curves than to see her walk away.

"No," he said, earning him another surprised face.

Her mouth dropped open and he was moving before he even realized it. Hayes came to stand beside her chair. With one hand on the back of the chair, and one hand on the table, he caged her in and leaned down slightly. "I like how you tried to protect me from the big bad slamming door."

"If you're just going to mock me—"

"I'm not," he clarified. "I haven't been attracted to a woman in a long time."

She blinked, those long, dark lashes briefly shaded her doe eyes. "And what do you expect me to do with that information?"

Damn she had a mouth on her. He liked it.

"I don't expect anything, but just as you are up-front and honest, so am I."

Her eyes studied him, more his mouth than anything. She was tempted, that much was obvious. She'd been tempted the moment she'd turned to greet him in the stables, but she'd been too ladylike to not keep her thoughts to herself.

Hayes was excellent at reading people. Well, not his ex-fiancée. He hadn't seen that coming.

"Well, Hayes," she drawled out and made every nerve ending in his body stand up and beg for attention. "As much as I'd love for you to rip your clothes off me and have your wicked way, I'm afraid I live in the real world and that's just not something I do."

Even though she delivered an impressive verbal punch, he had to give her credit. She managed to say that and sound sexy at the same time.

"I don't either, darlin', but there's always a first time for everything. Isn't that the old saying?"

Alexa pushed to her feet, forcing him to step back slightly. But he didn't move too far. Her body slid against his. He fisted his hands and willed all of his control to step up and assist a brother out. He couldn't resist this woman and her sarcasm and the way she called him on everything.

"I recognize PTSD."

And there went the arousal he'd had since meeting her.

Hayes turned away and headed to the kitchen window above the sink. He'd rather watch the rain come down in sheets than address the proverbial elephant in the room that his brothers had badgered him about for weeks.

"My grandfather had—"

"Enough."

He hadn't meant to yell, but damn it, he wasn't going to be analyzed. Not by his brothers and sure as hell not by this stranger he was more attracted to than he should be.

Hayes was well aware what he suffered from and giving it a label wasn't going to fix the issue. At some point, he'd have to go talk to someone, to bare his soul and give up all the demons in his mind that he'd lived with for years.

The electricity flickered once more, but remained on. Hayes continued to stare out into the yard where it stretched to the river. Puddles were forming in the grass and the waters in the river rolled quicker than usual. They were in for a hell of a storm and Alexa wasn't going anywhere anytime soon.

"Why don't you get flashlights," she suggested. "We better be prepared for the worst."

Prepared? He nearly laughed. He knew full well that there was no preparation for Alexa of the raven hair and mouthy chatter. She'd hit the nail on the head when she'd thrown out PTSD. Little did she know, others had tried to heal him and had failed.

What made her think she could come in here after knowing him only hours when his brothers who'd known him his entire life hadn't been able to get anywhere? Alexa might be the sexiest woman he'd ever seen, she might have a smart mouth, but she wasn't going to do any psychoanalyzing. If she wanted to do anything regarding this sexual tension, he'd be totally on board with that.

This was going to be a long, long night.

Five

Well, clearly the topic of PTSD was off the table. Alexa wouldn't make the mistake of bringing that up again. The man knew he had it—just as she knew. What level of hell did he live in on a daily basis? Did he just battle all of this on his own?

Alexa didn't know his brothers. Well, she'd seen Beau Elliott in movies, but that didn't necessarily count. From the way Hayes spoke about the others, he had a support system right here. Was he not ready to reach out? Perhaps he was too proud?

When her sister had passed, Alexa's father had a difficult time accepting help from others. But then he'd realized that was the only way he'd be able to move on and heal not only himself, but also his family.

"Tell me about your movie-star brother," she tossed out.

Hayes let out a humorless laugh. "You really know which subjects to hone in on to get on my bad side."

"Then maybe you should get me a list of safe things to discuss because I've yet to see a good side."

The glare he shot her suggested she should keep quiet, and that grouchy demeanor might work on some, but not her. She wasn't worried.

"Maybe we should try to get along during this storm and skip the getting-to-know-you portion of the night," he growled.

She thought about that for a second, but opted to ignore his request.

"I'd rather play the game," she countered. "I mean, I am wearing your clothes and it doesn't look like I'm going anywhere anytime soon."

Hayes shook his head, clearly not on board. "How about we get flashlights and candles? Then maybe I'll tell you about my renovations."

She pursed her lips and tipped her head to the side. "Sounds like a good idea to me. I can give you some tips."

"Did I ask for tips?" he countered.

Alexa crossed the room and patted his cheek. "Consider it my payment for your Southern hospitality."

"I didn't have a choice," he muttered beneath his breath.

"Sure you did, but you chose to push your moodiness aside and step up as a gentleman."

Those dark eyes traveled over her. "I'm always a gentleman, Lex."

Something shifted inside her. "Don't call me that."

Scott had always used that as his nickname for her and no one had called her Lex in two years.

Hayes's dark eyes landed on hers. "Fine. Alexa."

The way her name slid through his lips as he drawled it out made her think of skin to skin and promising nights. However, there would be neither skin on skin nor a passion-filled night.

"Let's start in the bedroom."

She blinked, then smiled. "Lead the way, cowboy."

Hayes did move, but not to lead the way. He leaned in and came within an inch of her. So close, his warm breath tickled the side of her face.

"And for the record, don't pat me like a little boy again."

Swallowing hard, she eased her face back just slightly to look him dead in the eyes. "Believe me, Hayes, I definitely don't see you as a little boy."

He wasn't sure what was more nerve-wracking, the fact she followed so close behind as he led the way up to the second floor, or the way she'd volleyed that sexual tension back in his face.

"Do we need to do anything for your horses?"

Hayes reached the landing and turned to face her. "They're all right. I have hay and feed in the barn. They're just as comfortable as they'd be down in Colt's stable."

Alexa glanced around the second story and then down over the first floor. The balcony-style hallway allowed for a beautiful view with the window behind overlooking the property and the family room below.

"This is such a gorgeous house," she muttered as she crossed to the window. "I can't imagine ever wanting to leave if I had somewhere like this to call home."

She'd mentioned that before, but he wondered why she didn't just buy a place in the country. Unless she was one of those picky people who had vast dreams and a meager budget.

"It never gets old," he admitted. "This land means

more than money. There's loyalty, family, protection. Everything is wrapped up in Pebblebrook."

Alexa turned her attention back to him. "That's the most I've heard you say at one time."

"Maybe I only talk when I'm passionate about something."

The corners of her lips twitched. One of these times when she mouthed off or gave that mocking grin, he was going to put that mouth to better use. There was only so long a man could hold out. Besides, the sexual attraction wasn't going away. If anything, the tension grew stronger the longer she was here.

Maybe a little seduction would take the edge off. Perhaps kissing her and seeing where that led would have them both putting this time to better use.

"What else are you passionate about?" she asked.

"Bourbon, fighting for what I believe in, good sex." Her eyes widened and Hayes nearly smiled. "Oh, come on. You can't be surprised by my answer, darlin'. I'm a guy."

"I guess I didn't expect you to throw the word *sex* down so easily."

With a shrug, he started down the hall that led to his master bedroom. "Sex has to be easy. Anything else implies commitment and that is impossible."

Alexa tipped her head and studied him. "Who hurt you?"

She just had to keep pressing. He'd almost rather have her pity than for her to dig deeper into his scarred heart. "My fiancée and my CO were having an affair behind my back."

Alexa gasped. Clearly, she wasn't expecting such honesty, but he wasn't sugar coating. Perhaps the bold statement would get her to back off and stop trying to pick his mind. If she persisted, he'd have to pull out the nightmare. Bringing it into the open would surely get her to back the hell out of his personal space.

"Trust doesn't come easily," he added. "Which is why sex is sex and anything more is meaningless."

"That's pretty cold," she told him.

"If you didn't want the truth, you shouldn't have asked."

There was no point in discussing this. They were completely different people and he wasn't here to make friends or make her feel good by opening up and spilling his emotions about the big, bad, scary things he carried in his mind.

The house tour was a safe subject, though he was a fool for starting in the bedroom. Unfortunately, that was the only area he'd completed.

He'd taken part of the wall in the hallway out to make room for the double doors leading to the suite. This house would be revamped from top to bottom, inside and out, but he still wanted to keep the charm of the '40s, when it had been built. No expense would be spared and he would put in high-end everything, but doing it himself was imperative. Hayes needed to stay busy, needed to be working with his hands. Idle time would only feed the devil that threatened him daily.

Hayes reached for the doorknobs and eased the doors wide open. Alexa's gasp behind him was all the validation he needed. Even his brothers hadn't seen the completed room yet.

"This is…" Alexa moved past him, her gaze traveling all around the room. "It's breathtaking and so perfect for an old farmhouse."

She crossed the wide-planked wood floor and stopped at the edge of the gray rug. Hayes moved on into the room, shoving his hands in his pockets and waiting for her to finish assessing.

Her bare feet padded over the rug and to the end of his king-size bed. "That wall of old boards is amazing."

"Those are from the original flooring that was in here. I'm reusing as much as I can to keep the place authentic, but still adding in the best fixtures and modern amenities like heated floors, lights and blinds on timers, security with motion cameras. There's so much to do in each room, it will definitely take some time."

Family and heritage meant something to him. Actually, it meant everything because at the end of the day, that was the only thing keeping him sane. After what happened overseas, if he hadn't had a sanctuary like Pebblebrook to come home to, Hayes knew he would've lost his mind.

Alexa took her time going between the built-ins he'd refinished, to the fireplace with original detailing and scrollwork extending up to the ceiling, and the wide window with custom-built seating and storage beneath. The crown molding had been refinished and he'd also kept the ceiling medallion and painted it white to match the rest of the clean lines.

After several moments in silence, Alexa turned to face him. "This is so impressive. All the detail, all the original touches that make this still feel like a farmhouse, but more up-to-date. The colors aren't what I'd have expected you to choose."

Intrigued that she'd given this any thought, Hayes hooked his thumbs through his belt loops. "And what did you think I'd do in here? Black like my soul?"

She tipped up a corner of her mouth and lifted her brows in silent agreement. "Or maybe a little happier, like charcoal to match your eyes."

Before he could question her on her reasoning, Alexa spun in another circle. She froze when she spotted the pocket door across the room. "The bathroom is in here?"

Taking off without waiting for his answer, Alexa slid the door open and gasped another surprise. "Hayes, oh my word. It's gorgeous."

He stayed back, though he knew she found the soaker tub on the far wall when he heard her delight. He'd purposely placed it right in front of the wide window. Not that he took baths, but it would make for a relaxing spot at the end of the day.

The oversize shower, big enough for four people, at least, caught her eye next. There was the pale gray tile on the floor, the original sinks he'd revamped by putting them in the old dressers from the spare bedrooms. They were mismatched, but painted the same crisp white. Still the farmhouse vibe with a touch of flair.

"Expecting company?" she asked, pointing to the shower.

He met her sly grin with a shrug. "You never know."

"I'd probably never get out of that tub if this were my bedroom."

"I'm not much of a bath taker unless I need to work out my muscles after a hard day, but a bathroom like this calls for a giant tub."

Her smile transformed into something soft, sweet. "Mason loves baths."

Mason? Hayes crossed his arms over his chest.

"Your boyfriend takes baths?"

Alexa's soft laugh filled the spacious room. "Mason is my son. He's fourteen months old."

She pulled her cell from her pocket and swiped the screen. "He's all boy," she beamed, showing him an image of a little guy with her dark eyes and olive skin tone. He sat in the middle of a pile of dirt wearing nothing but a diaper and boots. "He loves playing outside and getting messy, so bath time is just another adventure."

Alexa went on and on, flipping from one image to another. Her entire demeanor had changed and she was positively beaming as she talked about her son.

Her son.

Hayes hadn't seen that coming. That would explain her questions and trying to dig into his world. She was a nurturer by default and thought she could legitimately help him.

That was a big hell no and now that he knew the status of her personal life, that definitely changed the dynamic. This was the first he'd heard mention of a child…and most likely why she'd worried about her cell phone earlier.

Alexa being a single mother was a complete game-changer. That was reason alone for him to keep his hands to himself, but add her motherhood to his screwed-up life… Yeah. He needed to run fast and far, but he was stuck right here with temptation personified for the time being.

The last thing he needed was to get involved, on any level, with a woman with a child. He was messed up enough as it was, but to put any of his darkness onto an innocent child? No. Hell no.

"You're holding up remarkably well for someone who is stranded away from her son."

Moisture gathered in her eyes as she dropped the phone to her side. Apparently he'd said the wrong thing. He wasn't exactly known for his people skills. Which was just one of the many reasons he kept to himself.

"This is my first time away from him," she admitted, tipping her chin up and blinking back tears. "My friend

Sadie forced me to take a solitary vacation. She's the one who booked my long weekend at the B and B and she's babysitting. I don't know what I'd do without her."

Hayes didn't have friends like that. He had his brothers. That was all the support he needed. Friends, and fiancées, weren't reliable. At one time, he'd believed those in his inner circle were everything to him, but now he knew better. His eyes had definitely been opened, his heart hardened.

Maybe he shouldn't have been so gruff with Alexa earlier. She obviously missed her child and now she was trapped with a virtual stranger.

"Two of my brothers have kids," he found himself saying. "They're interesting. I don't know much about them other than they play and make a mess."

Alexa smiled. "That sums it up. Being a mother is the most important job I've ever had."

Hayes nodded. What could he say? Being a parent was never going to be a job for him. Good for those people who wanted children and took the time to nurture them, but Hayes could barely care for his own peace of mind, let alone a child's.

And he knew now that "Uncle Hayes" was around, Colt and Nolan would want him to be involved. Family was important to the Elliotts, but Hayes wasn't so sure he was the best role model for his twin nieces and nephew. Dealing with babies wasn't exactly something he was taught while he'd been jumping out of planes.

The rain continued to pelt down hard on the tin roof, which should have made for good sleeping weather. But if his demons didn't keep him awake, then Alexa being there would.

The flash of lightning and a hard clap of thunder put a viselike grip around his throat and squeezed. Hayes flung himself across the room and tackled her to the floor, sending her phone sliding across the tile. Instinct had him shielding her and taking the brunt of the fall. Pain shot through his leg.

He opened his eyes, focusing on how close Alexa's face was to his. There wasn't pity in her dark gaze, but understanding staring back at him. He didn't want to know what had occurred in her life that she could comprehend this level of hell.

"So doors and thunder." She shifted her weight off him, but put her hands on his cheeks. "What else do I need to look out for while I'm here? I don't want to trigger anything."

She wanted to cure him—those motherly instincts obviously kicking in. He didn't want to be mothered. He lived in the real world where he was permanently broken.

Sex was fine. But she was easing her way into his mind with expert grace.

Damn it. She was getting to him. The way she'd spoken about her son with obvious love had him admiring her even more than before, but that wasn't a mental green light to act on his attraction. Loyalty and family were so engrained in his life, how could he not appreciate a mother's love for her young son?

But she was here. Right here, touching him. Damn it. Resisting her was damn near impossible, no matter what common sense kept telling him.

Hayes's hands slid down her sides to rest on her flared hips. Silence settled heavily between them, but she continued to stare, waiting on him to reply. He could think of so much more to do than get into this discussion.

"Tell me," she urged, smoothing his hair away from

his forehead before sitting up. She sat next to him on the bathroom floor as if this were the most normal way to converse. Reaching for her phone, she clutched it like a lifeline…which it actually was. "I'm not judging, Hayes. I'm not mocking you or anything else. I care."

He snorted and came to his feet. "You just met me. You don't care."

Carly had cared. His CO had cared. Look where that had gotten him.

"You think because we just met today that I can't care?" She jumped up and blocked his path out of the room. Those dark eyes searched his face. "I make a living caring, wondering how I can make people's lives easier. I don't have to know you to question how I can help. It's human decency."

Needing to get away from her expressive eyes and delicate touch, Hayes eased around her, not at all surprised when she sidestepped to block him once again. This woman could drive him absolutely mad in so many different ways.

"Nothing you can do."

Crossing her arms over her chest, she gave a curt nod. "Fine. Then I'll just go out on the porch and watch the storm. I always loved a good storm anyway. It's relaxing."

When she spun around with that chin tipped up and those shoulders back, Hayes reached for her arm. Alexa stilled, but didn't look back.

"Civilian life is still an adjustment," he admitted. "Believe me, if I thought you had some magical way to help, I'd let you. But in reality, you're just here because you're stranded and probably in a few hours, you'll be back next door at my sister-in-law's B and B. Our paths won't cross again."

Alexa glanced back, her now dry hair shielded half her face. "I may not be magical, but that doesn't mean I can't help. You shut me down before giving me a chance."

Sliding loose from his hold, she left him standing alone in the bathroom. That woman was something. No, she was more. She was intriguing, sexy, compassionate...a mother. That last trait was something he had to keep reminding himself about. It made her even more off-limits. Hadn't he just seen at least ten pictures of her posing with her son? She had a normal life to get back to and he was just a blip on her radar.

There was so much that made up this intriguing woman. He found each layer appealing, even her being a mother. Because being a single mother could be difficult. She had to be strong and courageous.

Damn it all. He didn't want to discover any more layers to Alexa. He needed to stick with sexy and curvaceous. Physical traits were all he should focus on. There was room for nothing else. If she thought she could help him, she'd try again before she left. He had no idea what she did for a living, but from the way she touched him, the way she'd looked into his eyes just now, and the hurt in her tone before she left, Alexa truly believed she could do something for him. His brothers thought so, too. But they were living their own lives with their own families.

Raking a hand down his face, Hayes decided to see if Alexa's clothes were dry. Much more of seeing her parade around in his shirt was certainly going to cause him to reach his breaking point.

Six

"I'm not going anywhere anytime soon."

Alexa came into the laundry room doorway and watched as Hayes folded clothes in a precise manner. She'd gotten a text from Sadie just a moment ago with a picture of a very happy Mason hugging his stuffed horse. That horse never left his side. Even though Alexa knew he was fine, seeing a picture eased her mind.

"Texas storms can turn nasty fast," he stated as he creased another basic white tee.

"The river is up quite a bit," she told him. "If it doesn't stop raining soon, nobody will be going anywhere."

He froze. "It's not that bad already, is it?"

Easing back, she glanced to the clock on the kitchen wall. "It's already late afternoon. It's been raining for several hours and with the rain we had the other day, that river is really flowing and rising fast. When I checked the weather on my phone, it said the storm isn't going to be passing quickly."

Hayes muttered a curse under his breath. Alexa shifted out of the way when he pushed forward. Taking long, quick strides, Hayes went to the back door and headed out. Even in his panic, he closed the screen door with ease. He'd clearly trained himself, making his actions second nature.

Alexa went out to the porch as well, wondering where he'd gone. Since she hadn't put shoes on, she didn't want to go far. Stepping onto the wet stones leading to the barn, she raced toward the opening to see the barn empty, save for Doc and Jumper. They were staring at her without a care in the world. Where had Hayes gone?

Now soaked once again, she turned to the wide doorway and spotted Hayes at the edge of the river, hands on his hips, clearly not caring he was utterly soaked. The rain continued to come down in sheets and Alexa had no idea why he just stood there as if waiting for some divine intervention to solve their problem.

Unfortunately, there was no solution to Mother Nature's wrath. They were at the mercy of the elements… and this sexual charge that continued to surround them.

Finally, he turned, head down against the wind and rain as he marched back to the house. Alexa raced ahead and met him on the porch. Hayes raked a hand over his glistening black hair and flung the water aside, then he lifted that dark gaze to hers. And that's when he gave her a visual lick worthy of curling her toes.

The electrical current that had enveloped them since early this morning continued to sizzle and grow. She was powerless, captivated by a man she'd just met, yet she felt as if she knew him on some deeper level.

Hayes's eyes seemed to take her in all at once and Alexa knew exactly how she looked. Drenched, with his clothes plastered to her body, nothing beneath to hide the fact she was both chilled and aroused. She'd never been a fan of her curves, she definitely had her mother's build, but the way he was eyeing her—like she was the most desirable woman he'd ever seen—well, that made her not want to cover up and hide.

What would be the point? He'd already seen and she wasn't going to play the game of pretending to be shy. She was taking in her fill as well because Hayes had a body that would make any woman drop her panties and beg. Alexa wasn't most women and she was still determined to hold on to this thread of control and pray she wasn't here long enough for it to snap…because it wouldn't take much. His clothes were just as molded to his body as hers were to hers and he had some impressive muscle tone, glistening from the rain beading up on his skin.

"You should've stayed inside," he growled, remaining on the other end of the porch.

"I didn't know if you would need help with anything."

Those eyes ran over her again as he slowly closed the gap between them. "What did you think you could do?"

That question, delivered in such a low, gravelly tone did nothing to squelch her desire. This was crazy. She'd just met the man, yet he did something to her that she couldn't quite put into words. Granted, right now, she was having a difficult time with any coherent thought other than *take your shirt off, cowboy.*

"I have no idea," she admitted. "But I don't want you to think I can't help."

He took a step closer, never looking away from her eyes, her mouth. "Your clothes are all wet again."

"They're your clothes," she countered. Why did her voice come out so breathy?

The corner of his mouth tipped up. "Yours are dry now if you want to change."

She pulled in a deep breath, her breasts brushing against his chest. Had he closed the distance so tight or had she stepped forward? She'd been so mesmerized by his voice, his predatory gaze.

"Are you changing?" she asked.

Hayes reached behind his back and jerked the wet shirt up and over his head, tossing it onto the wood porch with a heavy smack. Tattoos covered his chest and up one shoulder. Dark hair glistened all over his pecs.

"You're not playing fair," she told him.

"Who said I was playing?"

He thrust his hands into her hair and covered her mouth before she could take a breath. Hayes's body leaned over hers, tipping her back slightly, but one large hand came around and flattened against her back, pushing her further into his strong build.

Alexa had never been so turned on and caught off guard at the same time. She gripped his bare shoulders and opened to him. There was no gentleness, nothing delicate in the way he kissed her. This was full-blown hunger and held so much promise of a stepping stone to something more.

"You're driving me out of my damn mind," he muttered against her lips. "My shirt molded to you is killing me."

"Take it off."

Where had that come from? It was one thing for him to take his shirt off, but she'd just ordered him to remove hers. What on earth was she thinking? This wasn't like her. Well, the blunt honesty was, but to be so brazen about her wants with a virtual stranger was completely out of the norm.

Those dark eyes seemed to go even darker. "Don't say things you don't mean."

Squaring her shoulders and taking a step back, Alexa found a boost of confidence and bravery as she reached for the hem and eased the shirt up and off. She threw it on the porch next to his.

"I never say something if I don't mean it."

And then he was on her. Strong hands gripped her waist and lifted her up. Her back hit the side of the house. Her breasts smashed against his chest. Locking her legs around his waist, Alexa ached in places she hadn't thought even worked anymore. It had been so long since she'd felt any desire, let alone given in to it. But Hayes sure as hell knew exactly how to make her feel, make her want and ache and tingle and all of the fantastic things that came with being aroused and out of control.

Whatever this temporary situation was, count her in. It wasn't like she'd see him again after she went back home and for once in her life she was going to be completely selfish and live in the moment.

Alexa arched against him as his lips found her neck and traveled down to her chest. Thrusting her fingers through his hair, she ignored all the reasons why this was not a smart idea that were swirling around in her head.

They'd been dancing around the tension for hours. So what if she wanted him? She was human, she had needs, and damn it, she'd never needed like this before.

Hayes shoved a hand between them and slid it into the oversize waistband of her pants. With no panties on, the access was easy as his fingertips found her most sensitive area.

Crying out, Alexa clung to him even tighter. His

hand moved over her, in her, and there was no way she could prevent the onslaught of ecstasy that overcame her. He muttered something in her ear a second before he nibbled on the sensitive spot on her neck.

Alexa's entire body tightened as she bowed, closing her eyes and letting the wave of ecstasy consume her. Hayes moved right along with her, slowing as she began to still. He didn't let up until the final tremor ceased. When he eased back, Alexa instantly felt cold and reality came crashing back. The rain, the storm…she was half naked on the back porch of a brooding billionaire's house and she'd just had the orgasm of her life.

Hayes continued to stare at her as he eased away. That hard stare, the heavy breathing and his chest rising and falling all indicated he'd not been unaffected by her pleasure.

He took an uneven step back.

"We should get inside."

From the tone and the slight gap between them, she knew he didn't mean taking things inside to finish where he'd left off.

What had happened in the last few moments? Whatever battle he faced internally had settled itself right between them.

He'd come at her like a man on a mission and she'd been the only one satisfied. Was he just going to go on like he wasn't miserable and aroused? Because she could see for herself he was both.

"That's it?" she asked, bringing her arms up to shield her bare chest. "What was that?"

"If you have to ask, I did things wrong."

Alexa continued to stare before she marched around him and grabbed their discarded shirts. She tossed his at his chest with a wet slap, cursing him in Spanish words her mother would've never allowed.

"Oh, you did things wrong," she agreed as she went inside, still careful of the door. "You claimed you weren't playing games, but you sure as hell just did."

Hayes remained on the porch for a few minutes after Alexa had gone inside. Somewhere between seeing her with his shirt molded to every wet curve and having her come apart in his arms, he'd had realized he was going about this all wrong.

And he spoke fluent Spanish, so he knew exactly what she thought of him at the moment. He wasn't too pleased with how he'd handled things either, but lust had overridden common sense and he'd been selfish. He'd needed to see her come apart; he'd wanted to be the one to make that happen.

From the moment he'd seen her in the stables, Hayes had imagined her writhing beneath him. He'd been set on seducing her. But the more time he spent with her, the more he learned about her, the more he wanted her and the more he knew he shouldn't have her...which meant his thoughts became even more jumbled.

She was a single mother. He might not know Alexa well, but he already knew enough to realize she wasn't the fling type. She had her life together and certainly hadn't taken a getaway to have some heated affair with a broken cowboy.

Hayes had vowed to get his act together. Of course that mental declaration came just as he was giving an orgasm to his temporary roommate.

Just because he was a mess didn't mean he had to make his unexpected guest miserable. It wasn't Alexa's fault he wanted her, but had issues of epic proportions.

It wasn't her fault the mere mention of kids put fear in him because he didn't want to get involved on any level with a woman with a child. Hell, he shouldn't be getting involved with a woman at all until he got his life together...if that ever happened.

The betrayal he'd experienced had scarred him, probably more than the hell he'd lived through during his tour of duty. Not that he was looking for a relationship or anything with Alexa. He had a need, a craving he hadn't experienced in so long, so he thought he'd act on it.

But she was a mother. A single mother. She was worried about being away from her son and here Hayes was worried about his hormones. They couldn't be more opposite. Sexual attraction was a fickle battle to fight.

And right now, he was a jerk. He'd nearly consumed her on the porch, taking what he wanted and leaving her little room to argue. Oh, he could tell she enjoyed his touch, but now what? He'd pushed her away because he had no clue what to do next, but she was stuck here, so he would have to face her at some point.

He was about as personable as that damn screen door he wanted to scrap.

Drawing in a deep breath, Hayes stepped inside the kitchen. Alexa wasn't around, which wasn't shocking. He'd be surprised if he saw her again while they were stuck here together. Most likely, she'd retreated to text her sitter or scroll through images of her son to keep her grounded and away from the big bad wolf.

Damn if he couldn't still feel her against him, though. He wanted her more than ever, but there was a line he shouldn't cross... Not until or unless he was certain she wanted...what?

There was a term for what he wanted and it was hot sex, no-strings, a one-night stand. But approaching Alexa with such crass words really didn't fit. There was something special, innocent about her and he shouldn't be trying to taint her.

Right now, the only thing he knew was that they were stranded together and the emotions were getting the best of them—or of him, at least.

He sure as hell had more than hormones to worry about. This water was rising. Their only saving grace, for now, was that the house and barn were up on a knoll that sloped down to the river and creek. But being surrounded on most sides was going to be a major problem if the rain didn't stop soon.

Since Alexa was not in sight, he shoved on the old work boots by the back door and headed out, sans shirt. He marched straight to the barn to check on the horses. If anything happened to Doc, Nolan would never forgive him.

His doctor brother had recently found his high-school sweetheart and had reunited. She'd been expecting another man's baby, which was a level of baggage Hayes never wanted to deal with. Between Nolan and Colt, both with their ready-made families, Hayes was starting to wonder what the hell was in the water around here.

The irony was not lost on him that he was now stranded with a single mom. Fate was tempting him or mocking, he wasn't sure which. Either way, he was getting damn uncomfortable.

Hayes checked the feed, refilled the water and decided to refresh the hay. Maybe something normal, some sort of manual labor would keep his mind off the fact Alexa had been panting in his ear and shattering against him only moments ago. He wanted to go straight into the house and finish what they'd started. His ache hadn't dissolved; if anything he wanted her even more than he had before he touched her. The way she'd come apart with such freedom and fire... He wanted more. If she was that open with her passion, how would she be once he got her into bed?

Her body hadn't been perfectly toned. Rather, her full hips, her soft abs were so damn sexy. She had the body of a woman with confidence and that was sexier than anything he'd ever experienced. Hayes wished like hell he could take his time and explore every dip and curve.

Again, though, they were total opposites and she wasn't looking for an affair with a stranger.

After staying in the barn for as long as possible, Hayes resigned himself to the fact that he was going to have to go inside and find her. Alexa deserved an apology.

Cursing on his way back to the house, Hayes had no idea how to go about this, but he knew no matter what he decided, he'd find some way to botch it up.

After stepping back into the house and closing both doors, he headed to the laundry room to change once again. He stopped short when he saw the clothes Alexa had been wearing. She'd taken her own things and left his draped over the drying rack.

Obviously she wanted to get out of the wet things, but all Hayes could think was that she'd wanted to be rid of him. The battle he waged with himself had slid between them and he didn't intend for her to be a target.

Already the darkness that plagued him was affecting others, and not just his immediate family. This should be reason enough for him to keep his distance from her, but he had to say something.

Now he had to figure out how the hell to make this up to her because neither of them were going anywhere anytime soon.

Seven

Given the fact Hayes had been a bastard, Alexa took it upon herself to explore the rest of the house. She'd texted to check on Mason again and got a picture back of him napping cuddled on the sofa with the infamous horse. At least one aspect of her life was normal.

Wandering around with her thoughts in a stranger's house wasn't helping her get over what happened on the porch.

If her body would stop tingling, that would be great. She was having a difficult time being so angry with Hayes when every part of her was still extremely revved up and ready to go. She didn't even have to concentrate to be able to feel him against her.

Alexa stepped into what appeared to be an office, but the cover on the couch and the stale scent told her this room had been neglected for some time. She wondered how long he'd been in the military and how long this house had sat empty. A room like this would have a story to tell and be rich with history.

The wall of shelves drew her in even farther. She adored reading, though lately it was more books about the ABCs or colors and shapes than anything. Which was fine, she loved snuggling with Mason after he'd had a bath and just before bed. They would settle in his room in the corner rocker and read and sing. It was actually the most relaxing part of her day. She wanted traditions and routines for her son, so he always felt safe, protected, loved.

Alexa blew out a breath and tried not to get too upset about being stranded here, away from Mason. She would've been away this weekend anyway, but now there was a real threat she'd be away even longer than the weekend.

The far wall of windows reaffirmed her fears as the rain beat against the side of the house. Alexa chose to keep her eyes on the books and something that would take her mind off her current situation. Surely there was one title in all of those she would find interesting.

The dust on the shelves was thick enough she doodled a heart. Wait. What? No, no hearts. She swiped her fingertips over the juvenile design and focused on reading the spines.

"Hope you like history."

Alexa cringed as Hayes's voice washed over her, but she didn't turn to face him. "Better than any other way to occupy my time," she muttered.

"I deserve that."

Alexa laughed, still staring at the titles as if some self-help book on dealing with cranky, sexy cowboys would jump out at her. "Oh, you deserve more, but I'm holding it in."

"Why? You've been brutally honest up until now."

True, but just because he'd been less than hospitable didn't mean she needed to be rude. Besides, she truly didn't know what to say. This situation was so far out of her comfort zone, she didn't even know what zone she was in. She was well aware that anything that happened here was temporary because she wasn't about to get involved with anyone and take them home to her son, but she'd never done temporary before.

"Are you going to look at me?"

Of all the times she'd wished for a snarky comment, now Alexa's mind came up blank. She blamed the intense encounter on the back porch for her momentary lapse.

"You don't use this room much," she commented casually as she shifted to examine more titles. "This is every reader's dream. A wall of books, a view out the window, a couch to curl up on. Not that I have downtime, but if I did, this place would be perfect."

"This was my grandfather's study. It hasn't been used since he passed."

Alexa turned now, crossing her arms over her chest. He'd changed his clothes, and thankfully put a shirt on. His hair was still damp, as was hers, but he looked... exhausted. Not merely tired, but absolutely worn down, almost beaten and defeated.

A piece of her softened because she truly had no idea what Hayes had gone through. If he'd open up just a little, maybe she could help. Then again, they'd just met and someone like Hayes wasn't about to bare his soul. She'd bet her entire year's salary that he'd been appointed a counselor through the military and had balked at talking to a professional. Someone like Hayes would think he could get through the difficult times on his own, or maybe he'd enlist the help of his brothers. But he was strong and determined, and not about to admit any type of weakness.

Hayes took a step inside the room. "What happened earlier—"

"Won't happen again."

He stopped a few feet from her and lifted one dark brow. "Is that right?"

"I'm pretty positive, considering the way you backed away from me."

Not to mention the fact that she hadn't missed how he'd closed up when she'd flashed images of Mason. Some men just weren't interested in children. Which was fine, it wasn't like she was about to take Hayes home or anything.

Hayes's lips quirked into a grin. Damn that man for being sexy and for making her want him. He'd touched her, kissed her, teased the hell out of her, and that orgasm hadn't done a thing to rid her of this desire. Now she wasn't just fighting attraction—she was trying to fend off the memories of how amazing he'd made her feel.

"Darlin'." He took another step closer "I set out to seduce you."

"Really? You have a terrible way of going about that."

He stopped just beside the cloth-covered sofa and leaned a hip against the arm. "You threw me for a loop when I saw you down in the stables and then to have you stranded here didn't help. But seeing you in my clothes, the way they plastered all over your curves, made me snap."

"How is that a problem?" she asked, her heart revving up all over again at his bold declarations. "I thought we were both on the same page."

He shook his head and glanced down to his hands. "We were until my mind started lying to me again and I went to war with myself."

Alexa padded across the hardwood toward him. "Don't be so cliché to say 'it's not you, it's me.'"

"My entire life is a damn cliché," he snorted. "You recall my fiancée and my CO, but I'll save you the sob story. In this instance, though, it was me. Damn it, I still want you, but…"

He shook his head and glanced toward the windows, where the rain skewed the view.

"You can't leave that sentence hanging."

Those dark eyes came back to hold her. "You don't seem like you'd be happy with a fling and I would honestly be using you to fill a void."

He'd be using her? Did he know how long it had been since a man looked at her the way he did? Did he realize that in the past two years she hadn't taken an interest in anyone at all and everything about him had her practically begging? She'd been turned on well before he made her come apart, and now that she knew what he was capable of…well…

"You don't know what type of girl I am," she countered. "No, I don't do flings, which should tell you something, considering I want you, too. But standing around chatting about it isn't helping either one of us. We're stuck here, we're attracted to each other and we're adults with our eyes wide open."

"What do you suggest?"

Alexa knew it was a risk, but she kept her eyes locked with his as she pulled her tank over her head and clutched it at her side.

"I suggest you finish what you started and quit worrying. Do you want me or not, cowboy?"

* * *

Holy—

Was she really doing this? After the way he'd treated her and acted like a complete jerk, Alexa stood before him wearing her lacy bra and hip-hugging jeans. With that midnight-black hair flowing around her shoulders, framing her mesmerizing face, she held all the power. His resolve had evaporated…if he'd truly ever had it to begin with where this vixen was concerned.

What was it about her? Her looks were definitely striking, but there was so much more. Her no-nonsense attitude, the vulnerability she tried to hide, her compassion he kept pushing away while she thrust it in his face anyway.

"Alexa."

She raised a brow and propped her hands on her hips. "I've seen the way you look at me, Hayes. I know this isn't some fairy tale or promise of commitment. We're adults, we're stranded, we're attracted. It's like the trifecta for a fling."

He laughed. Damn if this woman wasn't saying everything a man would want to hear. No-strings sex? What the hell was he waiting on? She'd already come apart in his arms, so he knew the desire was there.

Just because he was ready to rip the rest of their clothes off didn't mean he could stop worrying. She wasn't like other women who threw themselves into meaningless sex. He might have just met her, but that was one thing he knew for certain. So why him? Why now?

The Southern gentleman in him made him pause to assess the situation, but the Alpha male inside him was roaring to life and pumping with anticipation.

"Unless you've changed your mind—"

Hayes took one step to close the gap between them. Snaking his arms around her waist, he pulled her flush against him. "What do you think?"

"I think you better not go inside your head again and start thinking of all the reasons this isn't a good idea."

"It's not a good idea."

She trembled against him and threaded her fingers through his hair. "Do you really care?"

"Hell no."

He crushed his lips to hers, his need growing even more when she moaned and arched herself against him. Just one touch and the woman damn near exploded. He'd never been a one-night stand type of guy; he left that to his brother Beau. But if Hayes was going to have one, Alexa was perfect. She knew full well going in exactly what this was…and what it wasn't.

Hayes shifted his hands and gripped her backside, needing to feel her hips against his. She opened her mouth wider, taking more and giving just as much. Her fingertips trailed down and found the hem of his shirt. She tugged until he eased back just enough to be free of the unwanted garment.

When her hands went to the waistband of his jeans, Hayes gripped her wrists. "Protection."

Her lids lowered, her shoulders sagged as she blew out a frustrated sigh. "Obviously that's not something I carry with me, especially when I go out of town alone."

Disappointment rolled off her, but Hayes nipped at her lips. "My bedroom."

He might not have planned to be intimate since returning home, but that didn't mean he was a fool, either. And right now, he was beyond thankful he'd grabbed a box of condoms when he'd gone out for other necessities at the drug store.

A naughty smile spread across her face. "Then it looks like we're in the wrong room."

Hayes lifted her against him, forcing her to wrap her arms around his neck and legs around his waist. "Don't worry. I'll make sure you get where you need to go."

Those expressive eyes darkened at his veiled promise. Hayes flattened his palms against her backside as he left the study and turned down the hall to head toward the steps.

"You can't possibly carry me up there."

He nuzzled the side of her neck. The scent of something floral combined with fresh rain drove him out of his mind. Everything about this woman got under his skin.

"I can and I will."

"What about your leg?"

He gritted his teeth, hating there was any flaw to consider. "It's fine."

Alexa jerked her face back. "I'm not a lightweight."

"Neither am I," he countered as he reached the base of the steps.

"Put me down."

His firm hold on her tightened. "I'll not only carry you up, my knee will hold, I won't be winded and I'll still have plenty of stamina for other activities. You're welcome."

"I've had a baby," she continued to argue. "I'm seriously not as light as I used to be."

Hayes started up the steps, his eyes never leaving hers. "I don't know what you felt like before, but right now you feel pretty damn perfect."

Alexa pursed her lips as if she were biting back another argument. There was no way he was going to let her think for one second that she was less than perfect. Alexa fascinated the hell out of him.

Once he reached the top landing, he smacked his lips to hers. "You're still a lightweight," he informed her.

"How did you climb those stairs that fast carrying me?"

She sure knew how to stroke his ego. "I'm a former paratrooper. We're strong by default."

"A paratrooper? What exactly—"

"Is this something you really want to get into now?" he asked, taking long strides toward those double doors leading to his massive bedroom.

"No." She framed his face with her hands and slid her mouth over his. "I'm not really interested in talking at all."

He kicked the doors open with his foot and crossed the space. Right now he didn't care about the rising waters, the flickering electricity, the fact that they might be stranded for a while. He wouldn't mind being holed up with Alexa. Being alone would give him the opportunity he'd been waiting for to finally get her in his bed and take advantage of her lush body.

Hayes had even managed to block out the thunder that coupled with his PTSD to threaten his sanity. All he cared about was Alexa, about seeing her come apart in his arms again, because the sampling he'd had was not near enough.

Maybe she was the drug that could help him...temporarily of course.

Hayes stood at the end of the king-size bed and eased her down. When she lay back, he took a good, long look at the woman spread out before him. He'd never had a woman in this bed, hadn't given it much thought. He'd been so consumed with occupying his time and his thoughts with the ranch, but having her here was definitely helping him stay distracted. Who knew a perfect stranger would be the one to start healing his brokenness?

Alexa watched as he unfastened her jeans and tugged them down her legs. The plain white panties were more of a turn-on than any lingerie. The flare of her hips, the softness of her rounded belly and the fullness of her breasts straining against her lacy pink bra had Hayes rushing. He could do slow later…because there would be a later.

Alexa sat up and reached around to unfasten her bra. There was no way he would stop now. The sultry temptress displayed on his bed was more than enough motivation to ignore all the reasons why this was not his smartest idea.

All of this was temporary. The housing situation, the feelings…his lover.

While Hayes kept his eyes locked on Alexa, he stripped out of his clothes. In seconds, he retrieved protection from the nightstand and had it in place. The urgency spiraling around them had him rushing…but later, he vowed. Later he would explore that body because he already knew once would not be enough to exorcise her out of his system.

Alexa met his eyes with her heavy-lidded gaze as he came to stand between her spread thighs. Taking control, she reached up to grip his shoulders as she pulled him down on top of her.

"I think you need to take charge," she whispered. "I don't want any setbacks right now."

Damn. His heart clenched and that was the dead last thing he wanted. She got him. She understood the beast he lived with in his own mind. But he wasn't about to get too attached or emotionally wrapped up in how perfectly she understood his demons. There was no space for anything other than physical.

But taking the lead now that he'd finally gotten her where he wanted her was exactly what he'd been hoping for.

"That makes two of us, darlin'."

Alexa shifted her knees up by his hips and wiggled to get closer. "Don't make me wait."

Bracing his hands on either side of her face, Hayes joined their bodies, earning him a low groan and the sexiest arch from that sweet, luscious body beneath his. He might be physically in control, but right now she was getting into his head, overriding all the ugly to give him something akin to hope.

This was just sex, he reminded himself as he closed his eyes. He was taking every bit of this opportunity to use her sweetness to drive out his pain. No matter how temporary, he would welcome it.

Alexa framed his face, forcing him to look at her. "Stay here," she commanded. "Don't look away."

Yeah, she definitely held all the power here and he wasn't going to complain. Not one bit.

Their hips moved in perfect sync and she never let her eyes waver from his. There was a level of comfort with her he'd never found before. Finding something so rare had him drawing from her, using her in this moment.

When Alexa's knees clenched tighter against him, Hayes leaned down and covered her mouth with his. He wanted them joined in every way possible. There wasn't enough—he needed more.

Hayes reached down, slapped a hand over her hip and surged forward harder, faster. Alexa cried out, breaking their kiss and squeezing her eyes shut.

"Look at me," he demanded, echoing her words. He wanted to see and feel every bit of her release. They were both drawing from each other and he didn't want that bond severed…at least not yet.

Swollen lips, heavy lids, Alexa came apart all around him, which was all it took for Hayes to follow. His body tightened, he clenched his teeth, gripped that hip and lifted her leg even higher. Alexa's fingertips trailed up his arms and over his shoulders. She threaded her fingers through his hair as his body slowly started to come back down.

After his tremors ceased, Hayes started to shift to the side, but Alexa locked her ankles behind his back.

"Wait," she murmured. "One more minute. I'm not ready for reality just yet."

Reality was a bitter bitch. He wasn't ready to face it, either. But getting too cozy with this lush, passionate woman wasn't the smartest idea. Forget the fact that she matched him perfectly in bed, but she'd also honed in on his deepest fears and still managed to calm him with little effort.

Hayes ultimately gave in to her request to stay just a little longer. When he rolled to the side, he pulled her with him and cradled her head in the crook of his arm. He'd never admit that his knee hurt like hell. This was worth the pain. *She* was worth the pain.

He wasn't getting comfortable all nestled here with her in his bed, his home. He *wasn't*. He was simply coming down from great sex. That's all. This wasn't snuggling or cuddling or post-coital bonding. Their bond had come and gone during their intense intimacy.

But when her hand slid over his chest, Hayes had to close his eyes, because the warmth and tenderness from this woman was climbing over that wall he'd erected.

What happened to the quickie he'd set out to have? The seduction he'd wanted since he saw her in the stables had somehow turned into lying in bed together in each other's arms. How had they gotten to this point?

The second he'd discovered she was a mother, he'd vowed to keep his distance emotionally. Unfortunately, his emotions were scraped raw, exposed and easily accessible. And Alexa knew exactly how to make him feel, how to make him think about all the things he didn't want rolling over in his mind.

She felt too damn good.

Just another minute. He'd hold her one more minute and lie to himself about how he didn't enjoy this precious moment with this precious woman… Because right now, he truly didn't want to be anywhere else.

Eight

Alexa grabbed Hayes's T-shirt and slid it over her head. She'd apparently fallen asleep in his bed, but when she woke up, he was missing…and the bed was cool. Had he waited until she'd passed out and slipped away?

Regrets already?

Her tank top was still down in the study, so she pulled her jeans on to go with the shirt he had folded on his dresser. The sky outside the window had darkened and the rain continued to pour down. Alexa's stomach growled as she padded through the room and into the hall. A light shone from the first-floor family room as she glanced over the balcony railing. Still no Hayes in sight.

Surely he wouldn't mind if she went to the kitchen to find something to eat. Other than coffee, she hadn't had a thing since she'd grabbed a granola bar on her way out to the B and B this morning.

Alexa gripped the handrail and froze. Had it only been this morning that she'd left her house?

This morning she hadn't even known Hayes Elliott and she'd already been in his bed.

The woman she was here at Pebblebrook Ranch was not the single mother, teacher of special needs preschoolers. It was like she'd completely transformed into someone else the moment she got here.

Never in her life had she thought of having a temporary fling. She'd been married, then once widowed she'd focused solely on her son and providing for him. Dating hadn't even been a priority, let alone sex.

Something about Hayes brought out a side of her she hadn't even known existed. She'd only been with two people in her life before today, and one of those people had been her husband.

Pulling in a deep breath, Alexa descended the stairs. Some yeast-like aroma hit her as she got about halfway down. Pans clanging echoed through the house. Hopefully whatever he was making had enough for two.

Nerves curled in her belly. She truly hoped this wasn't about to get awkward. As confident as she'd been before, well…that had all stemmed from desire.

Right now, she was back to boring Alexa. She could turn snarky at a moment's notice if she started to get too overwhelmed by the intensity—and Hayes was definitely one intense man, in bed and out.

The second Alexa stepped into the kitchen, all her nerves were gone, quickly replaced by another rush of arousal. Hayes stood at the stove wearing only denim on the bottom half and ink on the top. Mercy, who knew a half-dressed man at the stove could be so sexy?

Her bare feet slid over the old linoleum, landing on

a squeaky spot in the floor. Hayes jolted and focused his attention over his shoulder, eyes alert.

"Sorry," she told him. "I didn't mean to startle you."

His shoulders relaxed as he raked his gaze over her and she was instantly aware of how potent those dark eyes could be. Almost as potent as his hands.

"You like wearing my clothes."

Maybe she did. Or maybe she liked the way they smelled, like a rugged man. "My shirt wasn't upstairs."

His mouth quirked. "You could've come down without a shirt. I did."

Great. He wasn't in a funk brooding about regrets and being noble or some other nonsense that would make this situation extremely uncomfortable. She was already feeling nervous again because she'd stepped so far out of her element.

At least he was talking like this situation was no big deal. Because it wasn't…right? Just because her body still tingled, she wore his shirt and she wanted to do it all over again didn't mean anything. It *couldn't* mean anything.

"If I'd come down without a shirt, you'd ravage me again and then we'd never eat," she replied as she crossed to the stove to see what he was making. "I'm starving, by the way."

"Who said I wasn't going to ravage you again?"

Standing right next to him, her wearing his shirt and him with no shirt, seemed far too intimate. Much more than the act of sex. Add in the fact that he was cooking and this whole scenario took on a domesticity she definitely wasn't comfortable with.

She'd done family before…then her husband died and she was left raising a baby alone and trying to piece together her shattered heart. She wasn't looking for someone to fill the void. One day, she would put herself first and find a man who loved her. She wasn't afraid of marriage, but she certainly wasn't looking right now.

Then again, she hadn't been looking for a fling either, but here she was with her breasts brushing against the shirt of a man she'd only met hours ago.

"Calm down, cowboy."

She patted his cheek. The bristles along his jaw tickled her palm and reminded her of how glorious he felt tracing his lips all over her.

In a swift move, Hayes grabbed her hand. Then he took it and flattened it against his chest. "That's the second time you've patted me like a child. I wouldn't do it again."

She shivered because, as he left the veiled threat dangling, there was so much heat in his tone, in his eyes, she wanted to pat him again just to see what would happen. She had no doubt it would be glorious.

And mercy, those muscles beneath her hand had her wanting to curl her fingers in to get a better feel.

"What are you cooking?" she asked, sliding her hand from beneath his. Alexa leaned over and spotted a pot with noodles. "You cook something like that?"

With a grunt, Hayes turned back and picked up the spoon from the counter. "I'm thirty-four years old, Alexa. I'm a single man. I either needed to learn to cook or starve."

"Aren't you supposed to live on bacon and beer?"

He threw her a sideways glance. "Those are definitely staples in a single man's diet. Hell, any man's diet. But I also appreciate real food and my mother was the best at homemade chicken and noodles."

Surprised, Alexa stepped back. "You make homemade noodles? Like, with a rolling pin and everything?"

"I'm wounded you think I can't." He continued to

stir as she stared, until he finally said, "Okay, fine. I didn't make these noodles, but I can."

Alexa crossed her arms and leaned against the wall next to the stove. "Is that right?"

"I swear, ask my brothers," he exclaimed. "We all can. My mother insisted we know our way around the kitchen, because she wasn't raising men and future husbands who couldn't help in every room of the house."

"Sounds like a smart woman."

A faint smile danced around his lips. "She was the best. My dad never was the same after she passed. Hell, he's really not the same now."

"Does your dad live on the estate, as well?"

Hayes shook his head and dropped the spoon back into the pot. "No," he replied, turning to face her. "He's in an assisted living facility not far from here. He doesn't know who we are most days."

She hadn't expected that. She knew Pebblebrook Ranch was the biggest in the state. It was the pride of the area, and now that rumors were swirling about the dude ranch extension, she would've never guessed there was heartache beneath all of that wealth and power. The dynamic family that seemed to have it all suffered brokenness just like anyone else. Money couldn't buy everything.

"I hate to hear that," she told him. "Has he been suffering long?"

Hayes leaned back against the corner of the L-shaped counter. Resting his hands on either side of his hips, he gave her a tantalizing view of…well, his amazing self.

"When I came home last year for a brief visit, I could tell he was much worse, but this time…"

Hayes shook his head and didn't finish. Alexa couldn't imagine having either of her parents not know who she was. How crushing and life-altering that must be. Hayes truly battled quite a bit between the PTSD and his father's mental state. So tragic.

"I'm sure he'd be proud of what you all are doing here," she replied. "Clearly, your parents raised some powerful children. Tell me more about your brothers."

Hayes pushed off the counter and went to the cabinet to grab a couple of bowls. "Not much to tell. Nolan and Colt are in love and married with kids. The only time I see Beau is when his face is on the screen. That's all."

Okay. Clearly, he loved his family, but he had some hang-ups. Not territory she wanted to venture into, and he'd made it crystal clear she wasn't welcome into the personal side of his life. Probably best all the way around if they kept their emotions out of the mix.

She didn't think that would be much of a struggle for Hayes, but she was one to get attached. Between her job and raising a toddler, her emotions were always getting involved in the lives around her. Simply because she and Hayes had just met didn't make her any less compassionate toward him, his burdens and the family who no doubt loved him and wanted to help him heal.

Alexa had to keep reminding herself this was simple. Adults did flings all the time. Not her, but other adults.

"I wasn't trying to make this any more than what it is," she informed him. "I'm not asking to meet them, just figuring out a way to pass the time."

What time was it anyway? This had been the strangest day and she couldn't keep track between the storm making the sky dark, the midafternoon romp and nap session, and then not eating.

Hayes scooped out hearty portions and sat the bowls on the table. Then he grabbed a loaf of bread and started slicing it.

"If you tell me you made that bread, I'm going to force you to come home with me and cook because I burn microwave noodles."

"Hell no, I didn't make this." He laughed. "Nolan brought this to me the other day. It's from our favorite bakery in town."

"Sweet Buns?" she asked.

"The very one."

After he got everything on the table, including sweet tea, she held on to the back of her chair and stared at the intimate dinner. It was simple, yet…still intimate and so like when she and Scott first got married.

"You all right?" he asked, taking a seat.

Blinking back the burn in her eyes, Alexa kept her gaze on the intimate setting. It didn't seem all that long ago she'd set the table for her husband. They'd share a meal and conversation, taking for granted how simple and perfect their life had been.

Alexa swallowed the lump in her throat. She'd not mentioned anything about Scott. Bringing him out into this temporary fling would make all of this seem more real, or like she was fully ready to move on. She hadn't quite gotten there yet.

"We all have our demons to face, don't we?"

Hayes fisted his hands on the table and pulled in a deep breath. "Let's take our dinner elsewhere."

She tipped her head, clutching her hands in her lap. She was a guest in his house and she didn't want him to make adjustments simply because her own issues snuck up and had her in a chokehold.

"Where do you suggest we go?"

Hayes came to his feet, grabbed his bowl and drink and jerked his head toward the front of the house. "Follow me."

* * *

Hayes had no clue what he was doing, but he'd seen Alexa's white knuckles as she'd stared at the dinner on the table. He hadn't even asked what she'd been through in the past, but obviously something spooked her when it came to…what? Eating with him? Sitting down to a kitchen table?

She'd asked about his family a few times, so if he were to add the pieces together, he'd guess whatever plagued her had to do with her own family.

Regardless, Hayes was glad to get out of there as well because eating together in his kitchen was a different level of intimacy. Sex was one thing, but settling down to a dinner he'd made? Yeah, that seemed to be sliding right into that relationship territory he'd vowed to stay far away from.

And a relationship with a woman and a child? No. Because if he got involved with a mother, then he'd be involved with a kid. He just couldn't do that, not to an innocent baby.

Years and years ago, before he went into the Army, he'd thought of having a family of his own. He saw his wife here at the estate helping to raise their children. He imagined teaching them about ranching. Then reality and war and all the ugliness crept in and corrupted every pure thought he'd had about the picture-perfect family.

"In here?" she asked, standing in the door to the study.

Hayes pulled himself from his thoughts and gestured her in ahead of him. "You seemed pretty happy in here earlier. And that was even before you started stripping for me."

Alexa laughed as she crossed the open space. "It's a room full of books with a large window, and if it weren't raining I'm sure there would be a killer view. All I need is a chaise and I'd be set. There's nothing to be unhappy about in here."

She went to the large window that stretched across the exterior wall. The padded seating area beneath the window was where she curled up with her dinner, obviously more relaxed and comfortable than in his kitchen.

Hayes stood a good distance away, taking her in with her legs crossed, holding a dinner he'd made, wearing his shirt... Perhaps the kitchen table would've been a better choice. He'd thought a dining table seemed intimate, but that was nothing compared to having her curled up in the room where his father had spent so much time. This room held so much history and now Alexa had wedged herself inside like she belonged here.

She took a bite and groaned. Well, hell. No matter where they ended up, his body would stir at the low grumble of her approval. That was the same groan she'd delivered in his ear as he'd slid into her earlier. Was he seriously considering another round?

Hell yes, he was. Who was he kidding? He'd had a sampling of Alexa's sweetness and her passion and he wanted more. They were stuck here and keeping his distance from her at this point was pretty much impossible. Night was fast approaching and at some point they'd have to discuss sleeping arrangements.

He just had to get her on the same page as his plan. An affair for the duration of her stay? He didn't think she'd be too opposed. A woman who bantered as easily as she did, who paraded around in his clothes... Yeah, he could get her back into his bed.

"Are you going to join me?" she asked, glancing over.

Hayes crossed the room and sat on the window seat, but left a good amount of space between them. Their dinner and glasses sat in the middle, providing a flimsy barrier.

"Tell me you're not going to change this room."

He forked up a hearty bite. "I haven't thought about this one to be honest. This was my grandfather's office, then my dad's. I don't really have much use for it."

Alexa's eyes widened. "You don't have use for a room where you can read and relax? Do you even know how lucky you are to have something like this?"

"Believe me, I know exactly how lucky I am to have everything I do." Flashes of another life he'd led for years boomed through his mind. "Just because I have money doesn't mean I'm not grateful."

"Do you have a panel that slides open and reveals a secret room?" she asked, picking up her tea. "Because I have to tell you, if you don't, then I highly recommend putting that on your renovation list."

"Is that right? And what else would you do?"

Alexa took a drink, then set her glass down as she drew her brows in as if trying to come up with some ideas. "Are we talking what I would do or what you should do? Because one of us has a ton of money and the other doesn't and lives in a town house about an eighth of this size."

Hayes shifted back and brought his knee up onto the window set. "Pretend this is your house and money isn't an issue. What do you see?"

Her brows lifted as those dark eyes widened. A breathtaking smile spread across her face and for a second, his heart clenched.

"This is fun," she stated. "Okay, well I'd definitely have a tire swing and a tree house out in that large oak by the creek for Mason. I'd want his bedroom to be the one facing that same tree so he could see his play area."

Of course she put her son's needs first. Someone like Alexa wasn't going to instantly go for the glam. Her son was her life. A fact Hayes would do his best to remember.

"You've nailed the master suite," she went on. "I think for the kitchen I'd keep it separate from the living area. That gives it the farmhouse feel. But I'm different in that I don't like the open concept everyone else wants. Personally, I don't want to see the dirty dishes from my living room."

Hayes shrugged. "When you live alone, there aren't many dirty dishes."

Alexa eased back and rested her shoulder against the window as she brought both of her legs up and crossed them. "But we're pretending this is my place and I don't live alone. Believe me, we have dishes. And the laundry. I never knew such a little person could have so much laundry."

Everything in her life circled back to Mason. He admired her for her strength and independence. Clearly, she was a wonderful mother. There was something special about the bond between a mother and her son. Hayes would always carry the memories of his mother in a special place in his heart.

"So you'd want a nice utility room?" he asked, trying to focus on their conversation and not the parallels between Alexa and his mother.

"Definitely," she said with a firm nod. "I'd want the laundry close to the bedrooms so I didn't have to haul it all over the place. I think for the living room I'd want soft, peaceful colors. I'd want sheers on the windows that stayed open so I could see the land. I'd have windows that opened easily because there's nothing like an evening breeze."

As she spoke, she looked outside, but the rain continued to beat the house. Alexa seemed lost in her own fantasy, as if she saw beyond the rain. Was life that simple? Could he look beyond the storm and see the other side?

"I think the house calls for an old farm table in the kitchen," she went on. "Or at least a long bar where friends or family can gather and eat in one room. My parents don't live around here, so I wouldn't have many visitors."

She stared down at her plate as she continued. "Growing up, we were constantly hosting family for dinner. Not only on holidays, but just because. That's part of my heritage. My father's family came from Puerto Rico. We gather together and fix an insane amount of food. I miss having a big house that I can fill with my family and friends. Sometimes I like to get together with my friends from work."

"What is it that you do?"

The question slipped past before his common sense could stop it. He shouldn't ask such things. He worried she'd get the impression he wanted more.

But he hated that longing in her tone. Hated that she was missing her family and the bond that obviously ran deep. He understood that all too well.

"I'm a special education preschool teacher."

Of all the things she could've said, he didn't expect that, but on the other hand he wasn't surprised. Alexa was a giver, so a teacher of children with special needs definitely made sense. He hadn't known her long at all, but he knew those kids were damn lucky to have a teacher like her.

"Sounds like a rewarding job."

A soft smile slid over her perfect mouth. "I love what I do."

And it showed in the way her eyes lit up and love laced her tone. There were certain things Alexa was extremely passionate about: her family, her son and her work. The similarities between them were starting to hit too close to home and he had to keep reminding himself they were stuck here and making the most of the situation. This wasn't some get-to-know-you start of a relationship.

"Working with children sounds terrifying."

"Says the man who served overseas," she retorted with a wide grin. "What did you do? Or can you tell me?"

"I was a paratrooper in the US Army."

When her brows rose, his ego volleyed up a notch. "You jumped out of planes and you think a room full of children are scary?"

With a shrug, he came to his feet and closed the space between them. "We all have our talents," he said, taking her hands and pulling her to stand before him.

"What are you doing?"

Hell if he knew, but he was going with his gut. Okay, he might be leading into this with another body part, but he wanted this woman and why should they deny it?

"Figured I'd show you more of my talents."

Her lips quirked up as she looped her arms around his neck. "Lead the way, soldier."

He reached to his back pocket and pulled out protection. "I grabbed it when I left the bedroom earlier. I wasn't sure where I'd want to ravage you again."

Dark eyes went from the foil wrapper in his hand back to his face. "Sure of yourself?"

Hayes lifted her off her feet and headed to the covered sofa. "Hell yeah, I am."

Nine

Alexa toweled off and slid into another of Hayes's shirts. She found herself becoming more comfortable in his clothes than her own. He'd definitely delivered on those promised talents, both in the study and in the shower.

Now he was outside assessing the rising water and checking on the horses. He'd made her promise she wouldn't come out because there was no sense in both of them getting soaked again.

She made him promise that if he needed help he'd come back and tell her and not be so hardheaded. Alexa worried with the storm still raging that the thunder would thrust him back to the darkness inside his mind, but she had to let him go on his own. She wasn't his keeper. She wasn't even his girlfriend, so hovering was not going to fly with this sexy cowboy. Besides, once she left he'd be on his own to handle matters his way.

Two stubborn souls trapped together proved to be quite the tug-of-war.

Yet they matched each other in bed and out. She shouldn't be thinking of all the ways they blended and complemented each other, but she couldn't help herself.

Alexa padded barefoot back into the bedroom and started adjusting the covers. Her body heated all over again as she recalled exactly what they'd done here hours ago.

But her heart clenched as night fell and she worried about Mason. Even if she'd been next door at the B and B, nighttime would still be difficult. She'd laid out his favorite book for Sadie to read him after his bath, but Alexa just wanted to hear his voice.

More than likely this separation was more difficult for her than for Mason. He was probably playing, watching his favorite cartoons and keeping Sadie on her feet.

What she and Hayes had going on was as simple as it was complicated. Bringing her son into the mix, other than just speaking of him and showing off pictures, was just another layer of intimacy that probably wasn't a smart idea.

This was all so temporary. She definitely wasn't ready to bring anyone home to meet her son or step up to play Daddy.

"The rain has slowed."

Alexa glanced over her shoulder. Hayes came into the room wearing nothing but his boxer briefs. "You lose your clothes in the rain?"

He hooked his thumbs in his briefs and stripped them off as well. Oh, mercy. That man had some serious confidence, and for good reason. All of those well-defined muscles, lean hips, broad shoulders, the smattering of hair across his chest, and that ink she'd all too happily traced with her tongue earlier… Honestly, if she looked half as sexy as he did, she'd parade around naked, as well. Alas, she had dips and curves and dimples in places that were not attractive. Yet Hayes made her feel exactly the opposite. And desired.

The man definitely made her feel desired.

"I put my clothes in the utility room since they were soaked. Figured you wouldn't mind."

"Not a bit." She crossed her arms over her chest and tried to calm her heart. "What are we doing, though?"

He continued coming toward her. "I plan on messing up that bed you just straightened."

Those big firm hands slid around her waist. Every time her body lined up with his, she couldn't help but think how perfectly they felt together. Why did something so temporary feel so right, so comfortable?

Were her mind and her hormones playing tricks on her? Even though it had been a couple of years since she'd become a widow, was Hayes the rebound guy?

"I'm not asking for more, but this is all we are, right?" she asked. "After I leave, we're done."

The muscle clenched in his jaw as he lined their hips up and palmed her backside. "But you're not leaving yet."

If he was trying to throw her off by dodging her question, it was working. "Do you ever get tired?" she joked.

He nipped her lips. "Oh, I'm tired. I plan on crawling into this bed and holding you until I get my stamina back."

Her heart ached. She hadn't slept in a bed with a man other than her husband. "Um…maybe I should sleep in the spare room."

And that was really saying something about her fear

of becoming too attached or pretending to play house. The man was wearing nothing and she had on only his shirt as he ground against her…and she was making plans to sleep elsewhere.

"Is that what you want?" he asked, easing back to look her in the eye.

Alexa swallowed. "I have no clue, to be honest. I haven't slept in the same bed with a man since my husband died."

Something dark slid across his eyes. "I wouldn't make you do anything. You want to sleep somewhere else, then I'll get the bed ready. You're in control here."

Was she? Because this all felt eerily out of control and spiraling into something she was neither ready for nor could wrap her mind around. Since meeting him in the stables, everything had snowballed. It was almost like she was watching this all happen to someone else.

Placing her hands on his shoulders, Alexa stared at the difference between their skin tones, hers dusky and his lighter. They might be completely opposite in their lifestyles, their upbringings, pretty much everything. But Hayes seemed to get her, to understand her need for space, and how could she not find that even more attractive than just the physical package?

"Why don't we watch a movie? Could we do something simple like that?"

Raking his hands up her sides, pulling the shirt with them, he let out a soft laugh before stepping back and dropping the material back in place.

"Sure, on two conditions."

"What's that?"

He nodded toward the bed. "We lie right there and you wear nothing."

Alexa opened her mouth, but Hayes held his hands

up, palms out. "That's all. Anything that happens beyond that is your call."

"You think we're going to lie there naked and nothing will happen?"

Hayes leaned forward enough to brush his lips against hers. "I said you were in charge. I never said nothing wouldn't happen."

Yeah, well, there was only so much a woman could take and Hayes had already proven he was well beyond her breaking point.

"You fight dirty," she muttered as she turned toward the bed and jerked the T-shirt over her head.

She was treated with a smack on her bare backside and a deep laugh.

One hour later, the movie still hadn't captured her interest. How could it? The man was not playing fair. Oh, he hadn't so much as touched her. He remained across the king-size bed with the sheet draped over his hips, just low enough to torment her. He'd propped pillows up and crossed his arms behind his head, showcasing ripped arms and a mouth-watering chest.

But even when the oversize footboard procured a gigantic flat screen at just the touch of a button, she still hadn't been able to concentrate on anything other than the dangerous game they were playing.

At the time, she wondered if he was just going to lie there, but he'd put on some new movie she'd never seen and hadn't said one word. Not one. He hadn't looked her way or "accidentally" brushed a hand in her direction.

For the past hour, Alexa had lain on the other side of the bed with an ache. Her bare skin slid over his sheets each time she shifted. She was seriously trying to hold still. The last thing he needed was to realize just how much this little cat and mouse game affected her.

Fine. If he wanted to play, then she was about to bring her A game.

Alexa pushed the sheet aside and eased from the bed. As she crossed the room toward the bathroom, she didn't so much as look his way, but she most definitely sucked her belly in and attempted to look somewhat fit and sexy. Not an easy feat when the only workout she received was chasing her kids in the classroom and giving Mason piggyback rides.

From the corner of her eye, she noted Hayes's attention following her as she entered the master bath. Once inside, she stood there for just a moment and simply stared straight ahead at the large soaker tub on the far wall. She had nothing to do in here, but she wasn't going to just lie in that damn bed and let him drive her out of her ever-loving mind.

Bare feet slid over the tile floor behind her. Before she could turn, strong arms banded around her midsection. Alexa found herself hauled back against a very chiseled, very firm chest. She couldn't suppress the smile that spread across her face.

"I thought I was in control and calling the shots," she reminded him.

Hayes's lips nuzzled her neck, causing goose bumps to race over her skin.

"Oh, you did call the shots when you strutted by me," he murmured in her ear. "You lay beside me shifting those legs, trying to ignore that ache. So here I am."

She should've known he'd see through her. Still, if this was her punishment, she welcomed the discipline... she was on borrowed time, after all.

Hayes's hand splayed across her stomach. His other slid up to cup her chin and turn her head just enough to look at him. But she didn't get a chance before his mouth crashed down onto hers. That hand on her belly went lower and Alexa whimpered.

The moment he touched her where she'd been aching for the last hour, Alexa nearly slid to the floor. Her knees weakened as every one of her senses was assaulted in the most glorious of ways.

Hayes continued to stroke her, kiss her, drive her completely insane until her body tingled more as it climbed higher and higher. Finally, she jerked from the kiss and cried out. He murmured something as he continued to pleasure her and Alexa reached to the side to grip the edge of the counter.

Moments later, her body settled, but she wanted more. Damn him for touching her exactly the way she needed to take the edge off but still leave her craving more.

"We should be ready to finish that movie now."

Alexa spun around, ready to tear into him for such an asinine statement when she realized he'd been joking. The gleam in his eyes was part amusement, part arousal.

"You better finish what you started, cowboy."

Those rough hands came to her waist and lifted her up onto the cool vanity. "We both know who started this, darlin'."

She locked her ankles behind his back and he reached into a drawer to pull out protection. Clearly, as long as she was here, they were going to have to keep those packets in every room.

In no time, he was sheathed and joining their bodies. Alexa knew this was absolute insanity to be this attracted to a man she'd just met. Still, there was nothing that could stop her from taking all the passion he gave. It had been so long... Didn't she deserve a little selfish happiness?

"Stop thinking," he whispered against her mouth. "Just feel. Relax."

Their bodies moved together as if they'd been together for years as opposed to less than twenty-four hours. Hayes's hands roamed all over her, his lips made their own path over her heated skin. The pleasure he gave was all-consuming. Alexa had never felt so needy and fulfilled at the same time. The way Hayes continued to explore her as if he couldn't get enough wasn't something she was used to…and she was quickly slipping into something deeper than just a heated affair.

Hayes slid those talented lips up the column of her throat as her body tightened all around him. He nipped at her ear before jerking his hips faster and capturing her lips. Alexa held on to him as she let the euphoria sweep over her.

Beneath her hands, Hayes's shoulders tightened as he continued to assault her mouth. For a long time, they clung to each other and she wondered when they'd be finished with each other. Would it be when she left? Would she be out of his system before then?

She'd never favored one-night stands, but she had to admit this was a memorable experience. Life-altering, actually. Because she knew for certain the next time she took a partner to bed, she would demand more than she'd ever realized she'd wanted.

Hayes rested his forehead against hers and let out a low grumble of laughter. "You ready for that movie now? Because I sure as hell couldn't concentrate earlier."

Alexa eased back as much as she could to look him in the eye. "You're such a liar. You lay there like you were so enthralled without a care in the world."

That naughty grin she'd come to appreciate spread across his face. "I knew you'd cave."

Swatting at his chest, Alexa uncrossed her legs. "You came after me."

"After you paraded in front of the screen. I wouldn't be much of a gentleman if I ignored your invitation."

When he stepped back, Alexa rolled her eyes, hating the instant chill that fell over her bare skin. "I'm picking the next movie and you're going to watch it."

With a shrug, he replied, "Fine by me."

Alexa named a title, something old that was ridiculously unpopular and very rare. Hayes lifted his brows in surprise.

"There's only one other person I've ever heard mention that film," he told her.

She hopped off the counter. "Really? Who else?"

"My best buddy from high school. We remained pretty close even during my first deployment, but then we lost touch and he passed away recently."

Unease curled through her. There was no way. Absolutely not.

"What was his name?" she asked, almost afraid of the answer.

"Scott Parsons."

Alexa's stomach dropped, her heart twisted, all the moisture in her mouth dried up the second her late husband's name landed right between her and Hayes.

Now what the hell did she do? She'd slept with her husband's best friend and Hayes already had issues with trust.

Tonight was about to get even more interesting.

Ten

Somewhere between the bathroom and the movie, Alexa had mentally and physically checked out. She'd slept in the spare bedroom, claiming she wasn't comfortable sleeping with a man since her husband.

That was understandable. Hell, he wasn't looking for snuggles and whispered promises in the dark so he should be relieved at her decision. But he wasn't.

Hayes wanted her beside him so he could roll over and touch her, pleasure her when he wanted. He'd never been this way with another woman—not even his fiancée.

So why Alexa? What was it about this affair that had him craving even more?

When he'd been with Carly they just fell into everything because of timing, something he could see clearly after the fact. Hindsight and all that. They'd been stationed together, had fallen into an easy pattern of friendship, which led them straight to bed. Of course they'd snuck around, but once their relationship turned serious, with an engagement, they went to their CO and explained things.

Hayes hated how he must've looked like a fool from the start. All of those inclinations of marriage, family and settling down here at Pebblebrook were naive goals he'd once held close.

Between the war zones he'd jumped into and the shock from the betrayal, it was a wonder Alexa had even made it into his bed. He'd been the poster child for needing a distraction and the perfect storm literally landed her on his doorstep.

So what the hell had happened last night that had spooked her? They'd both agreed this was only temporary. She'd been even more adamant than he had.

On the flip side, Hayes should be relieved she wasn't in his bed when the nightmares hit. She'd already witnessed his waking demons—there was no sense in her experiencing them while sleeping, as well.

The next morning, Hayes stood at the kitchen sink sipping his black coffee and staring out at the riverbank. Well, where the bank used to be. The usual cutoff from the land to the water had shifted somewhat as the flooding came up to nearly the slope that led to his porch. The rain had stopped. The storm had eased sometime during the night.

Actually, it had come to a head at eight minutes after two. He knew because he'd lain awake staring at the ceiling. After another nightmare and a clap of thunder, his sleep had been nonexistent. More than likely he'd never get a good night's rest again, not with the demons constantly chasing him away from any type of normalcy.

The crashing overhead jerked him from his thoughts.

His eyes went to the ceiling as he set his mug on the counter. Whatever Alexa had done, it sounded as though something had broke and his gut tightened at the thought of her being hurt.

Hayes raced up the stairs and down the hall leading to the room she'd chosen on the opposite end from his.

When he turned the corner, Alexa sat on the floor, his T-shirt bunched around her hips, and one of his grandmother's antique pitchers, which had sat on the dresser, was in the floor in shards.

"Don't come in," she told him as she reached for the larger pieces. "Go get me something I can put all these broken pieces in. I just… I wasn't paying attention and bumped the dresser. I'm so sorry."

Her hands shook as she lifted another piece. Hayes carefully watched where he stepped and crossed the room.

"Put those down," he ordered. "You're going to cut yourself."

She sniffed and glanced up to him, unshed tears swimming in her eyes. "Just get me the trash so I can throw these pieces away."

Hayes took the three large chunks from her hand and set them back on the floor. Without warning, he lifted her from the floor and adjusted until one arm was beneath her knees and the other behind her back. He left the room with threatening protests from his houseguest.

"We'll clean it up later," he informed her as he went to his room. "Are you upset because you broke that piece? Because I don't even go in that room and my mother wouldn't want you to cry over broken porcelain."

Alexa swiped a hand over her face. "I'm not crying, though I am sorry I broke that."

"Your eyes are pretty watery. Must be allergies." He sat her on the end of his bed and picked up one foot to assess for any cuts. Satisfied there were none, he checked her other foot. "You're not cut anywhere. Let me see your hands."

Like the hardheaded woman he'd come to know, she put her hands behind her back and tipped her chin. "My hands are fine. I'm going to get dressed and ride Jumper back to the main house."

Hayes shook his head. "Not a good idea, darlin'. That low area on the property is swimming in water. Remember the spot I showed you when we rode through?"

Her chin quivered, but he had to hand it to her, she didn't give in to the emotion. "I want to get back to my son."

"How long were you staying at the B and B?"

"Two more days." She narrowed her eyes. "I can't be here that long."

Hayes crouched down in front of her. "Listen, I don't know what's got you so spooked since last night, but there's no pressure from me. If you're worried about my expectations, I have none. Do I want you in my bed while you're here? Hell yes, but I won't push you."

"That's not…" She shook her head and looked away.

Whatever she was dealing with was none of his concern. He didn't want to take on any more baggage from anyone. He could barely carry his own mess.

Hayes came to his feet and backed up. "Why don't you get your clothes on, or stay in mine, I don't care. Then meet me in the kitchen."

She brought her focus back to him, drawing her brows in and narrowing her eyes. "Why?"

"I've got something planned for both of us to take our minds off everything else going on."

When her eyes trailed over his body, he had to laugh. "As much as I'm tempted to give in to that silent invitation, I have something else in mind."

"I wasn't inviting," she stated.

"You said the same thing last night after you paraded naked in front of me. We know how that ended." He sauntered from the room and called over his shoulder, "You'll want pants and shoes on for this. Meet me downstairs in five."

Well, ten minutes later and she was in the kitchen, where Hayes was absent. What on earth was he doing?

Alexa went to the French press and figured she'd fire it up and have a good cup of coffee. It was so rare she managed to grab a cup at home. Mornings were usually rushed getting Mason ready for the sitter and her trying to get to school on time to be the smiling teacher ready to go when her students arrived.

"Taking your coffee break already?"

As the drip started, Alexa turned her attention from the much needed morning fuel to the man behind her clutching a sledgehammer.

"Um, what are you doing?"

"We're going to take down the cabinets."

Stunned at his bold statement, she leaned against the counter and crossed her arms. "Why are we busting them out? I didn't think you'd decided what to do in here, yet."

With a shrug, Hayes eased the sledgehammer on the floor and propped the handle against the door frame. "I know these need to come out before I can do anything else. So the first thing I'll do is empty them. Considering nearly every room in this house is bare, it shouldn't be difficult to find a home for the few dishes and pans

I have. And my microwave can go anywhere for the time being."

Alexa figured she had two options: she could drink her coffee and get going on this demolition or she could drink her coffee and spend the rest of the day worried about things she had no control over.

Either way, she was getting her liquid jump-start.

"Let's get these cleaned out then," she told him.

An hour later they had everything out of the kitchen and eating area. The counters were cleared off and Alexa was caffeinated and ready to go.

"Do you want to hit them first or should I?" he asked.

"I'll do it."

Hayes crossed the room and grabbed the sledgehammer. Before he handed it over, he pulled a pair of work gloves from his back pocket.

"Put these on."

She eyed the well-worn leather. "Where are yours?"

"I have one pair and you're wearing them. Not up for discussion."

She wondered if he ever wore gloves. Those strong hands of his were rough, but they slid over her skin easily and sent shock waves all through her.

If she didn't focus on the sledgehammer instead of those masterful hands, she'd knock herself out while doing this demo work. Without arguing, she slid the gloves on and adjusted the wrist strap. When she picked up the sledgehammer, she was a little surprised how heavy it was. She didn't do too many teardowns. While she had lived alone for some time now and did most repairs herself, she'd had no reason to own such a tool.

Though she did re-screen her back door and change out the leaky pipe in her bathroom faucet. She was rather proud of herself when she managed things on her own. Considering everything was on the Internet, she would at least try once before calling in reinforcements. She didn't always have the funds to pay someone to ride to her rescue when things went wrong.

"You got it?" Hayes asked.

Alexa nodded. "Where should I start?"

"Anywhere. As long as you don't bust the window, feel free to smack anything. I want it all gone."

She went to the side of the base cabinet and gave a swing. Well, in her mind it was a hefty swing, but it barely made a hole in the side of the old wood. How embarrassing considering Mr. Muscles behind her could probably take it out with one whack.

"Harder," he demanded. "Whatever you were upset about this morning, whatever came between us last night, use that emotion and smack the hell out of that cabinet."

Thoughts about how life wasn't fair ought to do it. The fact her husband had been taken, her child robbed of a father, then to find the one guy she was interested in had been her husband's friend...

The sledgehammer came around, her grip tightened as it made contact with the cabinet and busted right through.

Apparently channeling heart-clenching emotions was the perfect solution for demo work. She needed something to demo at home on those days that she struggled to get through.

"At this rate I won't have to do anything but haul everything away," Hayes joked. "Swing at it again."

Alexa banged over and over. The muscles in her shoulders and arms burned, but this was the greatest therapy she'd ever had. Even if she could get over that hurdle of Hayes's insistence about being alone, now she had the barrier of her late husband. How had she never known about Hayes?

Obviously, they'd lost touch after school when Hayes went overseas, but Alexa had never heard his name and—

Oh, no. She had. She'd heard his name several times. Well, she'd heard Scott talk about his friend "Cowboy." Ironically the same name she'd called Hayes right before they...

"Okay," Hayes called over the crashing sound.

Alexa took a step back. Sweat dampened her skin, causing her tank to cling. She eased the head of the sledgehammer down to the ground and rested the handle against her thigh. She was definitely going to feel that workout in the morning, or quite possibly tonight.

"Feel better?"

Alexa glanced over to see a very smiley Hayes. She hadn't seen that much emotion from him other than when they were naked.

"I'm sweating and sore," she told him. "That was amazing."

Hayes chuckled and stepped forward. "Maybe I should exorcise some demons, as well."

Alexa stepped far enough back to not get hit by the debris, but still close enough to admire that very masculine form in action. Muscles clenched and bulged as he took his own frustrations out. Before long, the entire wall with the sink was done.

Hayes stepped back and pulled in a deep breath. "Well, that didn't take as long as I thought."

"What about the other wall?" she asked.

"That's a gas stove, so I'll wait to pull that out. I think we've done enough for the day."

Alexa took in the carnage and propped her hands on her hips. "So how are we going to cook?"

Hayes propped the sledgehammer against the new-found wall. "I have plenty of things. We won't need to cook."

Alexa narrowed her eyes. "Like what?"

"Ice cream, cereal, bread from Sweet Buns."

"I'm here for two days and I'm going to leave fat if all you have is carbs."

Hayes's gaze raked over her entire body. "You're perfect now and you'll be just as perfect when you leave even with a buffet of carbs."

Words every woman wanted to hear. If she was ready for something more, maybe he'd be the one who helped her get back into life as a couple, the man who fed her every fantasy, the one she told her every secret...

Except, oh, that's right. She was now the one keeping a secret from him.

She couldn't tell him about Scott. Something about the admission felt too emotional, too raw. She'd be gone soon and Hayes would never have to know who she was. That was for the best, considering both of them had determined this to be physical only and nothing personal.

Bringing Scott into the mix now would only make it seem like she'd been keeping something from him all along. And considering they weren't going to see each other again, it was best she just kept her late husband to herself.

"I say we have ice cream for dinner," he told her as he closed the distance between them.

"You don't have to talk me into that if that's what you're thinking."

A corner of his mouth tipped up as he reached her

and banded his arms around her waist. "Oh, that's not what I'm thinking."

Alexa flattened her palms against his chest. "We're filthy, Hayes. And I know I smell."

His lips trailed over her jawline. "We're definitely on the same page. You do stink."

She swatted his shoulder with a laugh.

"Which is why I'm about to go scrub you from head to toe and work out those sore muscles in the shower."

She squealed as he scooped her up. She started to say something about his knee, but he wouldn't care. He'd ignore the pain and push through because once Hayes had his mind set on something, he followed through.

And apparently he had his mind set on making sure she was thoroughly clean.

Eleven

By the time Sunday rolled around, it was like the sky opened up and poured down some much needed sunshine. Alexa was sore in places she hadn't even known muscles existed—from the sex and the demolition. She'd ended up staying in Hayes's bed last night, though she'd vowed to herself not to. Things just progressed and that was where she stayed.

The man had a power over her she couldn't comprehend. It was as if the word *no* didn't exist where he was concerned.

And her time there had come to an end. She'd been in contact with Sadie, never once admitting where she'd truly been. They were expecting her home this afternoon and Alexa knew the water had gone down and she'd be able to deliver on that promise.

Alexa adjusted her tank over the top of her jeans. She was most excited about putting on different clothes.

Even though Hayes had washed her things while she'd worn his shirts, she still wanted something else.

But part of her hated to be leaving. The house was amazing and she wanted to see more of what would be done, but she'd never be back. She'd never see what happened with the kitchen they'd torn up and she'd never know if he put that long farmhouse table in for guests or if he'd keep it simple so he didn't have to invite people over.

So much about this house, and this man, she would miss.

Being in bed with him last night, not just the sex but the actual intimacy, had sparked something deeper inside her. After sleeping alone for two years, having someone right beside her had been...perfect. She'd slept so well, all cradled in Hayes's arms. When morning had come, she didn't want to get up, but she knew this fairytale couldn't last forever. The real world waited on both of them.

As Alexa came down the steps and headed toward the kitchen, she heard Hayes cursing.

"Something wrong?"

Her question had him jerking around, eyes wide. His hair was all a mess, from sleeping or running his fingers through it. "Just a minor electrical issue."

"Do you want to ride back with me?" she asked, knowing full well he would.

He pulled in a deep breath and met her gaze from across the space. "Stay."

That one word held so much power as it settled between them.

"You don't mean that."

Those dark eyes that held so much pain never wavered from hers. "You know I never say something I don't mean."

That was true. She'd come to know him pretty well over the past couple of days. "You'll be glad to see me go," she informed him, remaining where she was in the doorway.

"I slept better last night than I have in years."

She didn't want to hear that. She didn't want to know that she had an impact on him because last night had been a turning point for her, too. She was having a difficult time gearing herself up to leave. And if he were being honest, he wouldn't want her to stay. This euphoric state would wear off and he'd want his privacy once again. It was best for everyone if she left as planned and they forgot about each other.

In theory, that's exactly what should happen, but Alexa wasn't so quick to believe that she could just let all of this go.

"You'll do fine once I'm gone," she assured him, and tried to take the advice herself. "You only slept so well because of the sex."

Hayes shrugged. "Maybe so. I wouldn't turn down sex or a good night's sleep if you stayed."

"We both know that's not a good idea and I have a son and reality to get back to."

Now he did cross the room, and her heart kicked up. Maybe it was the whirlwind weekend or perhaps it was just the man himself, but every time he looked at her she couldn't help the fire that continued to blaze within her.

"Maybe I don't want reality," he told her as he nipped her lips. "One more day. Stay one more day."

The man could tempt a saint, and she was surely no saint. Alexa slid her hands over his arms and tipped her head back.

"You make me want to forget responsibilities."

That naughty grin from his lips had her biting back her own. "Don't look at me like that," she scolded. "I'll never leave here."

Hayes slid his hands under her tank as his lips captured hers. Easing her back, he completely covered her, but held her all at the same time. The man's strength never failed to impress her, which was just another reason she found him so intriguing.

Her time was up, but she desperately wanted to stay. She wanted to get Mason here to play in the yard and ride the horses. But that was all fantasy because the reality was Hayes was a billionaire living in a far different world.

As his lips pressed deeper into hers, Alexa clutched at his shoulders. Those fingertips brushed the underside of her breasts.

"Looks like everything is fine here."

Alexa jerked, but to Hayes's credit, he only cringed. He kept his hold on her, tipped back and all, and merely turned his head to the back door where a tall, broad man stood. He had to be an Elliott. He had the same dark hair, dark eyes and naughty grin.

"Get out, Colt."

Annabelle's husband. No doubt Annabelle wondered what had happened to her B and B guest.

"Is that any way to treat your brother who came all the way back here to check on you?" Colt asked, stepping farther into the room. He eyed Alexa. "Colt Elliott. You must be Alexa. My wife has been worried, but I told her if you were with Hayes, you'd be in good hands."

Pushing against Hayes, Alexa stood upright. "I was definitely in good hands, as you can tell."

Colt's brows rose as he let out a bark of laughter. "I didn't mean to interrupt."

"Yes, you did," Hayes growled. "Now leave."

"Actually, I was on my way out." Alexa turned her attention to Hayes for the briefest of moments before looking back to Colt. "I need to get to the B and B and settle my bill and gather my things."

"There's no bill."

Alexa spun around. "There is a bill. Just because I didn't stay there doesn't mean I don't owe."

"It's taken care of," he insisted.

Narrowing her eyes, she crossed her arms. "You're not paying my bill."

"It's taken care of," Colt repeated.

Turning back to the other brother, Alexa sighed. "Is this how it's going down? I'm getting overruled? I can pay my own way."

"I thought your friend was paying," Hayes asked as he came to stand beside Colt. She could definitely see the similarities now. "Why are you settling up?"

"She gave me the money to put on my card for the room, but I'm giving it back. She watched my son all weekend. That was enough of a favor."

"Well, consider your stay free and clear," Colt declared. "Annabelle was so worried, though we figured you'd gone out with the horses and since Doc was missing, we knew Hayes had taken him."

"Nolan's always too busy at the hospital or with his new wife and baby to get Doc out that often," Hayes added.

This familial moment was not helping her get out unscathed. She'd already fallen in love with this house; she'd partly fallen for the man, though she chalked the unwanted emotions up to the whirlwind affair. If she stayed much longer and heard more about their brotherly bond and witnessed their banter firsthand, she wasn't sure she could push aside what she was feeling for Hayes.

Oh, yes, he'd asked her to stay, but he meant in his bed. And, tempted as she was, she had to leave. Now.

"I can ride Jumper back," she suggested.

"Nonsense," Colt replied. "Why don't you take my truck? Hayes and I will get the horses back to the stables."

"Take your truck?" she asked.

"I'll drive her," Hayes stated. "In your truck. You can stay here until I get back or you can ride Doc. Leave Jumper for me."

"I can send a stable hand," Colt suggested.

"Jumper is fine here and I'll take—"

"I'll drive myself."

Both sets of eyes turned to her. Alexa cleared her throat and squared her shoulders. "That is, if you don't mind," she said to Colt.

"Not at all. Keys are in it. Just leave it parked at the B and B."

Hayes's dark eyes held her in place for only a moment before she crossed the room. The two men parted at the back door as she passed through. With her hand on the screen, she carefully let it close softly, so as not to bang.

Her heart clenched as she froze on the porch. She risked a glance over her shoulder where Hayes stood on the other side of the screen, his hands shoved in his pockets, the muscle in his jaw clenching.

She wanted to say something, anything, but with Colt only feet away what would she say? Even if they'd been alone, what words would fit this type of situation?

Thank you seemed a bit ridiculous, and she couldn't tell him *see you later* because they both knew that to be false.

With a brief smile, Alexa pivoted away and headed toward the shiny black truck in the drive. She didn't risk looking back again as she turned around and drove away. She didn't even glance in the rearview mirrors. She needed to make a clean break and forget how much her heart got wrapped up in this heated affair…and she needed to forget the fact she'd deceived him by not telling him the truth of her identity.

But they'd never see each other again, so she needn't worry. Right?

Twelve

"If you're going to sulk and be moody, then go home."

Hayes ignored Nolan's comment and patted Jumper's side. He hadn't ridden his horse in five days. Not since he'd brought her back after Alexa left.

Actually, he hadn't been down to the stables since then at all. He'd been doing some behind-the-scenes work for the dude ranch, contacting engineers to do some surveying since they'd decided to add another set of cabins on the west side of the property. Hayes was fine with that locale. Nolan could oversee it once it was up and running.

When he hadn't been working with the settings and contractual aspects, Hayes had spent many sweaty hours in his kitchen. But every time he'd try to demo or stand back and think exactly what he wanted, he saw Alexa in there. He heard her telling him about her family and the gatherings and how he should have a large table stretching down the length of the room.

"Go home."

Hayes glanced up at Colt's demand and found both brothers staring at him now. "I'm tending to my horse. If I'm offending you two, why don't you leave?"

Colt shifted his boots on the stone walkway between the stalls and crossed his arms over his chest. If he thought that would intimidate Hayes, that was absurd. Nothing got to him anymore.

Well, one person did. She'd gotten to him with her compassion, the way she spoke of Mason, the images he'd seen of how she held her son like he was the most precious thing on earth. There was so much love in a woman like that.

"Listen, we've given you space to deal with the hell you've endured. I know you don't want to talk about it, but since your houseguest left, you've been especially standoffish."

Hayes smoothed a hand down Jumper's mane and snorted. "How the hell would you know? This is the first time you've seen me in days."

"You ignored my texts and didn't return my call about the engineer's ideas," Colt countered.

"I've been busy."

Trying to sleep without Alexa.

How insane was that? He'd actually slept with her only the one night, but for some reason that was the best rest he'd had since he'd come home. Maybe it was the sex relaxing him, but he didn't think so. Alexa understood him. She hadn't pushed verbally, but emotionally she'd been there. They were virtual strangers, yet they knew each other in the most intimate of ways.

"What the hell happened?" Nolan asked, then held out his hands. "No, don't tell me. If you like her, why are you here?"

Hayes glanced back toward his meddling brothers. "I refuse to get into some locker room chatter. Whatever happened between Alexa and myself is between us."

"Annabelle said she was crying when she came back to get her things," Colt supplied. The concern in his eyes could barely be seen beneath the wide brim of his hat, but Hayes missed nothing. "I saw how the two of you were."

"You saw us kissing," Hayes corrected. "Don't read any further into it."

"After that." Colt uncrossed his arms and took a step forward. "I saw the way you two looked at each other, the way you stared after her when she left. Don't tell me it was all physical because I don't believe it."

Hayes stared for a second before he turned his focus back to his mare. "I don't care what you believe."

But he did care that Alexa was crying. He shouldn't care. He should just let her go. When he'd asked her to stay he'd had a moment of weakness, though he hadn't been lying when he'd told her it was only so she'd stay in his bed. That was precisely where he wanted her and five days later his need was just as strong, if not stronger.

"Have you been to see Father lately?" Nolan asked, thankfully changing the subject.

Hayes led Jumper back into her stall. "I was there yesterday. He didn't know me, but he knew my name. He kept referring to the time I fell into the river."

"You were eight," Nolan stated. "He's been in that time frame for a while now. I think that's where he wants to stay. When I'm there, he's always talking about Mom, but we're all very young."

Hayes hated seeing his father robbed of his memories, of his dignity. They'd gotten him the best care possible and kept the rumors about the Elliott patriarch at bay. Nobody outside the immediate family needed to know just how bad their father was.

As much as he hated seeing his once robust dad in such shape, Hayes made a point to visit every few days. He knew his brothers did the same and they tried not to go on the same days so as not to confuse him. The dude ranch had been his baby and no matter what happened with his health, the Elliott brothers would see this through…which was just another reason he didn't have time to get swept away in some affair.

The weekend was enough. It had to be.

"Pepper said Alexa came into the store yesterday."

Hayes shot Nolan a glare, to which Nolan merely shrugged.

"And how does she know Alexa?"

"Stone River isn't that large of a town," Nolan replied. "And nearly everyone has been in Pepper's shop."

Nolan's wife had opened a flower shop that also showcased her one-of-a-kind paintings. Apparently the store had been thriving since the grand opening last year. No doubt Nolan had a hand in helping to make sure his wife's venture was a huge success.

Hayes slid the stall door closed, then turned and hooked his thumbs through his belt loops. "Is there a point to this story?" he asked his brother.

Nolan merely smiled. "Just gauging your reaction."

Glancing from brother to brother, Hayes took his hat off and tapped it against the side of his leg. "This is why I rarely come down here. Being analyzed by you two is not my idea of work or a good time. I'm fine. Okay, I'm not, but I will be."

"Is this the war trauma or your houseguest we're

talking about now?" Colt asked, leaning against the stall on the opposite side of the walkway.

Hayes leveled his gaze. "All of it."

Colt nodded and turned away. Heading toward the open end of the stables, he called over his shoulder, "Annabelle has Alexa's address on file."

Hayes clenched his teeth as Nolan stared with that damn smirk on his face. "Shut up."

He didn't want his meddling brothers, or his sisters-in-law, getting in his personal business. Though apparently it was a little too late for that.

Without a word, Hayes spun on his booted heel and left the stables. He either needed to work on some more demo to get this frustration out of his head or he...

No. That's not what he needed to do. He'd cut ties with Alexa. He'd learned his lesson about getting tangled up with the wrong woman and Alexa being a single mother was definitely not for him. Not that he didn't love kids. He adored his brothers' children. How could he not? Two beautiful twin girls and a bouncing baby boy?

There was just so much evil Hayes had seen. All the nightmares he had, sleeping and awake, would not be a good atmosphere for a child. Being an uncle was a far cry from being hands-on with a child every day and if he and Alexa became involved, he'd want to be hands-on. That goal from when he was younger still lived deep inside him. The goal of a family, of children. But he'd had to ignore that need—he'd had to push it so far down it wouldn't creep up and make him realize he was missing everything he'd wanted for his future.

Hayes hopped into his truck and pulled up the drive leading to his house. As he passed the main house, Annabelle sat on the porch swing watching her twin girls playing at her feet.

A small tug of jealousy slithered through him, but the unwanted emotion had no place in his life. Growing up, he'd always thought he'd have a family and they'd all live here on the ranch. Then life happened and reality smacked him in the face with a sledgehammer.

He threw up a hand in greeting when Annabelle lifted her head and smiled as he drove by. His brothers may have found happiness, and he was grateful they were bringing up another generation of Elliotts for the next chapter in their lives.

But if anyone was looking to him to carry on the name, well, they were wasting their time. Hayes wasn't about to take over rearing a child.

"You are so rotten."

Alexa laughed as she settled Mason onto her lap. She sat on the stoop and held her son in one hand and the container of bubbles in the other. Well, the now empty container, since Mason had opted to dump the bottle down her legs.

Good thing she was barefoot and in shorts. Mason only wore his swim trunks and a little dirt on his feet from where he'd been running around in their meager front yard for a while. The postage-stamp-size yard was such a disappointment after seeing the spread on Pebblebrook.

Alexa groaned. That certainly wasn't the first time that ranch, or the sexy rancher, had flooded her mind over the past week. It had been seven days since she'd left and there wasn't a day that went by where she didn't wonder what he was doing, how he was doing. Was he sleeping? Was he still tearing out the kitchen?

"Play." Mason clapped his hands, then smacked her legs. "Play."

Alexa sat the bottle next to her thigh and wrapped her arms around his slender little frame. "You silly boy. You dumped all the bubbles on Mommy. They're all gone."

"No."

"Yes," she countered. "They're all gone."

Mason reached over her hold and picked up the bottle. Turning it upside down, he shook it. A few random drops filtered out, onto her leg once again, and his lip started quivering.

"More," he cried.

"How about we clean up and go to the park?" she suggested.

The park was about a twenty-minute drive, but it had a fabulous play area and a nice walking path where she could take him for a stroll once he tired of playing. That way he got a nap and she got a little workout.

Granted the best workout she'd had in ages was the sledgehammer to the cabinets.

And once again her thoughts circled back to Hayes. Why couldn't that man just leave her head? In such a short time, he'd embedded himself so deeply into her life she worried what would've happened had she stayed longer.

Alexa shifted Mason and came to her feet, holding him against her hip. "Want to go swing and slide?"

He nodded, despite the tears in his eyes. "Swing."

"Let's go get some shoes and a shirt for you," she told him. "Then—"

The words died as a big, black truck pulled into her short drive and stopped right against her garage door. She'd seen that truck. And the man inside it had haunted her dreams for the past week.

What was he doing here?

"Truck, truck, truck," Mason chanted.

Adjusting her hold on her son, Alexa hated that her first thought was how frightening she must look. She was wearing her go-to outfit: old cutoff shorts, neon yellow to really accentuate how wide her backside was, and an old white tank with paint stains.

Oh, well. He'd come to her so he was going to have to see her in all her tacky glory. No doubt he had on another pair of those hip-hugging jeans, a T-shirt that stretched across glorious muscle tone and that familiar black hat with a brim, shielding a most impressive set of black eyes from the sun.

The man just sat there staring at her. Well, she assumed he was. That hat shadowed half his face. Was he going to get out? Had he changed his mind about visiting her? Were they in some warped staring contest?

Mason patted her cheek, pulling Alexa from her trance. She smiled at her son, though her stomach was in knots. She'd needed to break from Hayes. As amazing as their time together had been, she had to keep her distance.

He had been her husband's best friend. Hayes valued honesty and commitment and after all he'd been through, she wasn't sure he'd be too happy with sleeping with his best friend's widow.

The second his door swung open, Alexa pulled in a deep breath and stepped down onto the narrow walkway leading to her portion of the drive.

As he rounded the hood, her heart clenched and she couldn't stop herself from raking her gaze over him. Indeed, he wore exactly what she'd feared and he was absolute perfection. These seven days apart had done nothing to settle that attraction rooted deeply inside her.

"What are you doing here?" she asked as he came closer. Not the friendliest greeting, but they'd agreed to be done.

"Seeing you."

He said the words so simply as if leaving his ranch wasn't a big deal.

"You never leave home," she reminded him. "Or that's what the rumor has been."

He nodded, crossing his arms over his chest. "Some things are worth leaving for."

Now, why did he have to go and say things like that? Why did he have to make this about more than physical? Because showing up unannounced at her home was definitely taking things to another level.

"Wait. How did you know where I lived?" she asked, shifting Mason to her other hip. "Never mind. I'm sure you just asked your sister-in-law."

Mason reached out toward Hayes's hat, but Alexa eased back. "No, baby."

"He's fine."

Alexa held on to her son's hand. "He'd pull your hat off and chew on it or throw it down."

Hayes took his hat off. "And that would be just fine."

He held the hat out to Mason. Alexa did not want this little bonding moment, no matter how harmless. Nothing about Hayes Elliott was harmless.

Not only had she gotten way too attached during those few days, she now carried a secret that would no doubt anger him and make him look at her with disdain and resentment. She'd rather not have that hanging over her. Hayes had been hurt enough.

Mason grabbed the hat and sure enough, the brim went straight to his mouth.

"Oh, Mason," she cried. "Don't do that."

Hayes's mouth quirked into a grin. "He's really fine."

Yeah, but she wasn't. Watching another man interact with her son...well, that was something she hadn't prepared herself for. Mason wasn't used to being around men. Alexa never dated, certainly never brought a guy to her house, and the babysitter was a woman. Mason didn't really have an adult male in his life.

And she sure as hell couldn't let Hayes into her son's life. The fragility of her heart where this man was concerned was simply too much. And he was in such a delicate state himself. No matter how amazing they'd been together, him showing up here was a bad idea.

"Why are you here?" she murmured.

"You already asked that."

Alexa lifted her eyes to meet his. "You never answered."

"I told you I wanted to see you."

She quirked a brow.

"Fine. What do you want me to say?" He put the hat on Mason's head and lifted her son from her arms. Shocked, Alexa watched as Hayes smiled down at Mason as if this were the most normal thing in the world. "Do you want me to tell you my sleep has gone back to hell since you left? That when I walk in my kitchen I wonder if you'd like what I've done? That I put up a damn tire swing because you mentioned it?"

Oh, no. This was even worse than she'd thought.

"We agreed—"

He held up his free hand. "Yes. We agreed to be physical. I miss the hell out of you, Alexa. I'm not here to ask for a relationship or even marriage. I want you and when I want something, I make sure I have it."

Mason ran his hands over Hayes's stubbled jaw. Back and forth, his little fingers raked over the dark hair along his chin. Alexa couldn't tear her eyes away. They were literally bonding right before her eyes and she couldn't do a thing to stop it.

"You can't just come here and expect me to… What? What do you think will happen now?"

Hayes strong hands held her son so tightly. "Come back to the house with me."

"No."

Those lips twitched again as if he were trying not to smile or laugh. It was great to see that emotion from him, but at the same time, she couldn't fall into that rabbit hole.

"Bring Mason. Play in the yard. That's what you wanted, right? A yard for your son?"

Alexa narrowed her gaze. "You're not playing fair."

He eased closer, his eyes dropping to her lips. "We've already established I'm not playing and I never said I was fair."

Mason turned his head, causing the hat to bump against Hayes's face and topple to the ground. Alexa quickly scooped it up and handed it back to Hayes before reaching for her son.

"We're headed to the park," she informed him. "So, if you'll excuse us."

He remained right where he was, unmoving, barely blinking. The way he stared at her with those dark eyes made her wonder if he could see into her soul. Could one broken person actually connect so deeply with another?

Alexa shook off the haunting thought.

"You get me," he stated, taking a half step closer. "Hell, I've only known you a week and there were ways you understood me better than my own family."

Swallowing, Alexa adjusted Mason as he laid his

head on her shoulder. Apparently he was ready for a nap, so maybe the park wasn't in their immediate future.

"That's not true," she argued. There was no way.

"Do you think it was easy for me to come here?" he asked. "I battled this for a week, but damn it, I want you to come back to my house. Just come for the day and I'll drive you back."

Alexa laughed. "This is absurd, Hayes. You're getting caught up in a moment that passed."

In a lightning-flash move, he snaked an arm around her waist and hauled her free side against him. "The moment didn't pass. I still want you. I've been through hell, and when I see something or someone that will bring a semblance of happiness, I'm going to take it."

Oh, mercy, she wanted him, too. The fierce need she had a week ago had only grown and now he was here and touching her, looking at her with the same hunger as he'd had when they'd been stranded and naked.

"Bring Mason. We'll ride horses."

Alexa closed her eyes. He'd put himself out there and come to her. He'd shoved aside his fear of leaving the ranch. He was inviting her son to ride horses, which he'd never done, and he wasn't even close to backing down.

"Fine," she whispered. "We'll come. But I'm driving myself and I'm not spending the night."

Hayes ran his lips along her jawline. "We'll see."

The shiver raced through her and Alexa vowed to herself not to sleep with Hayes again. Not with the secret she carried. Maybe one day, when he healed and they were friends?

No, not even then. Someone like Hayes would see sleeping with his late buddy's wife as a betrayal. He could never know.

Thirteen

"You were pretty sure of yourself."

Hayes stepped into the stable by his house and threw a glance over his shoulder to Alexa. "I had the stable hands bring them up. If you hadn't come, the horses still could've stayed here."

He was a damn fool for bringing her back here, but it felt right. She felt right to have here. Not that he was thinking long-term or a commitment, but damn it, he was at a point in his life that if any happiness came his way, he was going to grab hold with both hands and to hell with the consequences.

He could even accept the bond he was forming with her kid.

Right now, he was going to take a ride with Alexa and Mason. The little guy was too adorable and when he'd reached out for Hayes earlier, he hadn't hesitated to take him. Children were so innocent, so loving, and that was something he'd quickly discovered when he'd gotten home. His nieces and nephew had calmed him and kept him grounded and sane at times. Having Mason here with Alexa, damn it…there was something a little too familial about it, but he hadn't been lying when he'd said he'd missed her.

And he hated that underlying vulnerability and loathed even more that she'd witnessed it.

"I'm still not comfortable around horses," Alexa commented. "So how should we do this? Maybe just set Mason on the saddle and let him pet the horse?"

Hayes slid open a stall and shook his head. "Nah. He can ride with me on Doc and you can take Jumper. We'll stay right around here so you're comfortable."

He tossed a thick blanket on Jumper's back and grabbed a saddle from the wall. Alexa's silence had him risking a glance her way. She chewed on her bottom lip as she held tight to her still-sleeping son. Apparently the kid could sleep through anything.

Hayes had held him while Alexa had changed earlier. He hadn't been opposed to the little shorts and tank she sported, but her jeans and T-shirt would be a better option for riding.

"I'll hold on to him," he assured her. "We'll go slow and he'll be just fine."

She smoothed Mason's black hair across his forehead and nodded. The kid looked exactly like her with that dark skin and coal-like hair. Even his eyes were dark as midnight. And her love for her son was so evident. Hayes knew she'd do anything to protect him. That family bond and loyalty ran deep in him too, so he knew full well how much Mason meant to Alexa. They were all each other had left.

"I want to talk to you about something."

Her eyes darted to his as she lifted her brows. Mason

stirred in her arms and she patted his back. "What's that?"

After securing the saddle, Hayes rubbed the back of his neck. "I have a thing I need to go to in a couple weeks and I need a date."

Why did he feel like a fool in high school asking out the homecoming queen? Probably because he'd never asked out the homecoming queen. He'd simply hopped in the bed of his truck after the game and flipped up her dress and lost his virginity. So…yeah, this was quite different, but he still hated the uncertainty.

No, he actually hated the whole ordeal he'd been faced with and the ceremony coming up. It was absurd, useless, and he was the least deserving person to be honored.

"I received a phone call from the governor a couple weeks ago."

"What?" Alexa stepped forward, her eyes wide. "The *governor* called you? You just throw that out like it's not a big deal."

He shrugged and eased Jumper from her stall. "It's not. I mean, they want to have a dinner and present some award for my service and sacrifice. It's completely unnecessary, but it's in two weeks and I want you to go with me."

Mason continued to stir until he popped his head up with a yawn. He glanced around, his attention landing on Jumper and the little guy immediately started clapping.

"I'd say he's ready for his first ride," Hayes stated. He lifted the rein and hung it on the hook outside the stall before moving to the next one with Doc. "Give me one second and I'll get my horse ready, then I can help you onto yours."

"I don't need help," she stated. "Can you get back to the governor and why I need to be your date?"

He quickly blanketed and saddled Doc. "I'd rather move on and we just agree I'll pick you up two weeks from yesterday at six. I guess I'll wear my uniform, so you'll probably want to wear a fancier dress."

"I don't—"

"Have one?" he asked, tossing her a glance. "I've already called in some favors and they're being delivered. Keep whatever you want. Keep one, keep them all. I don't care."

Hayes led Doc out and hooked his reins, as well. He patted the side of the stallion's neck, smoothing out the coarse mane.

"Would you slow down for a second?" she demanded.

Blowing out a sigh, he turned to face her. "Listen, I don't want to go. The award is absurd and the last thing I need is recognition. I didn't do anything overseas that any of my fellow soldiers wouldn't have done. I just happened to survive. I don't want to go, but I sure as hell don't want to go alone, because…"

Softening her facial expression, Alexa stepped forward and reached for his hand. "Because you don't like going anywhere?"

Shame and guilt slithered through him. "So you'll go?"

The silence settled between them. Mason lifted his hands toward Jumper and Hayes slid the boy from Alexa's arms.

"Right here," he told Mason, taking his little hand and laying it on the velvety part of Jumper's nose. "Soft."

He'd much rather focus on the horses, on introducing Mason to his first ride. There was something so magical about getting on the back of a horse and setting out for nowhere. Not a care in the world, no troubles followed him… Well, they did, but at least he was more at ease out in the pasture.

He'd also been at ease with Alexa lying next to him in bed. She might be adamant that she wasn't going to get between the sheets with him again, but he was just as adamant that she was. How could he give up on something that felt so perfect? On something that settled him in ways nothing else had in months?

Whether she liked it or not, Alexa was exactly what he needed, and wanted, right now. And he'd be damned before he let her just walk away because he knew full well she felt something, too.

"I'll go," she finally conceded. "But I'll buy my own dress."

"Already taken care of." He took her hand and led her to Jumper. "They'll be there on Wednesday evening."

Her lips thinned as she settled her free hand on the saddle horn. "You're arrogant."

"True," he agreed. "But I'll have a smokin'-hot date."

With a laugh and an eye roll, she mounted the horse. Damn if she didn't look good here.

But that was an image he'd have to get out of his head. Pebblebrook was his. At least this portion was. He wasn't looking for another woman to fill the void his fiancée had left. He sure as hell wasn't looking for a baby in his life.

He wasn't looking for anything more than what Alexa had to offer—sweaty nights and a sense of peace. He needed that, so he needed her.

Her vow to stay away and keep her feelings compartmentalized was shot all to hell. Somewhere between him showing her how perfect he was with her son and him swallowing his fear and asking her about the dinner, Alexa had slipped further into...

No. Even she couldn't say it to herself. There was no room for anything other than friendship. Okay, they'd slept together and now they were friends, but whatever. Anything more would be tragic...and simply asking for heartache. Hers and his.

Seeing Hayes with her son, riding through the fields, it had been too much so she'd kept her eyes on the horizon.

Now they were back at his house and he was making sure the horses were fed and watered. Alexa sat on the edge of the back porch and watched as Mason toddled around plucking up random grassy weeds. The tire swing swayed in the distance from a large, sturdy branch.

It was all Alexa could do not to peek inside the kitchen window. She was dying to know what stage he was in with the space they'd demolished. Knowing him, he hadn't sat around and done nothing inside there.

A large black truck moved slowly up the drive and Alexa came to her feet to gather Mason. She remained on the porch and watched as Annabelle stepped from the vehicle. Alexa didn't need to be spotted here; that would only be fodder for the family gossip mill. They all undoubtedly knew she'd spent the entire weekend here during the storm. And here she was again, this time with her son.

Annabelle hopped out of the truck, her blond hair swirling around her shoulders. She offered a big smile and a wave. Alexa returned the kind gestures, though her heart was pounding. How was she going to explain being back? It wasn't like she and Hayes were... What? Dating? Nope. They weren't even having sex anymore.

Friendship, that's all this was. And really, could their relationship even be labeled as friends? She kept an epic secret from him and he had hang-ups about life in general. She wasn't ready to have a man come into her son's life and Hayes wasn't looking for an instant family. They were going nowhere fast and there was nothing she could do but hold on.

Thankfully, Hayes stepped from the stables and crossed to Annabelle. Alexa really didn't want to have to make awkward conversation.

"What are you doing back here?" Hayes asked, a smile on his face as he accepted a hug from his sister-in-law. "Where're the girls?"

"Actually, Colt is home with them because he's been in the stable all night."

"What's wrong?" Hayes asked. "I had a couple horses sent down to me and never heard anything was wrong."

Alexa stepped off the porch and eased Mason back down into the grass. She tried not to appear that she was eavesdropping, but it was rather difficult to not overhear everything.

Annabelle waved a hand as she reached for the passenger-side door. "Oh, you know how he is. Since the vet told him that the new weanling needed extra care, he's like a worried father. But I got up this morning because I couldn't sleep without him there, so I made you some sticky buns and herb bread."

Alexa's mouth watered at the thought...and she gained five pounds just from this conversation. Carbs were not her friend. But Annabelle used her baking to her advantage and advertised that along with the B and

B. The two went hand in hand…or so Alexa assumed. It wasn't like she'd actually experienced anything the B and B had to offer.

No, Alexa had been taking advantage of what the mysterious Elliott brother had to offer instead.

"Good thing I brought extra, since you have company." Annabelle pulled the dishes from the truck and Hayes quickly took them from her. "Thanks. I can bring more later."

"No, she's not staying."

Alexa's shoulders stiffened. True, she wasn't, but he was awfully quick to dismiss her. Most likely that was for her benefit, since Alexa had been so adamant about not staying long.

But now that she was here, she wanted to. She loved watching Mason roam around the yard. She'd loved seeing him on the back of Doc and nestled against Hayes…but those were things she couldn't want and Hayes had made it abundantly clear that he wasn't looking for more.

She wasn't either, but she could see herself here. No matter how she'd fought it during their time together, she realized now that she could see herself with him—if there wasn't a secret settled between them.

Now she was going to a formal dinner with him and he'd managed to get dresses ordered for her. Did he know her size? Did he know that anything too form-fitting would only accentuate the flare of her hips and the roundness still in her belly from having a baby?

Alexa rubbed her forehead and smiled as Mason ran and toppled over. He got right back up and took off again, this time straight to Hayes.

Coming to her feet, Alexa started for Mason, but without missing a beat, Hayes scooped him up and held him in one strong arm while juggling the baked goods in the other.

"Let me take him," Alexa said as she neared. "We really should be going anyway."

Hayes shot her a look, holding tight to Mason. Instead he handed her the bread and buns. "Take these into the kitchen. I know you've been wondering what I've done in there."

Alexa narrowed her eyes, to which he merely quirked one dark brow. This was not the time for a standoff, not with his sister-in-law mere feet away, taking in the whole scene.

Taking the baked goods, Alexa turned to Annabelle. "Thanks. These smell wonderful."

"I hope you'll stick around long enough to enjoy them."

Nothing could be said to that, not without incriminating herself, so Alexa turned and headed for the house. Hayes knew exactly how to pique her interest...in more ways than one. But she wanted to see what he'd done inside. Then she would take Mason and go. The longer she stayed, the harder it would be to leave.

But the second she stepped inside, her mouth dropped. He'd not only gutted the room, he'd taken down the wall to the dining room. Dark flooring had been laid and right in the middle was an old farmhouse table that stretched so far, it could easily seat twenty people. There were no chairs or benches and the cabinets weren't installed, but there was a table.

Just like she'd suggested.

Well hell. Now what was she supposed to do? She wanted to keep her distance, but how could she? Everything he did—

The back door squeaked open and Alexa sat the

baked goods on the table before turning around. Hayes eased the door shut with one hand while holding on to Mason.

"What do you think?"

It was all she could do not to choke up at the heart-clenching emotions swirling around inside her. "I love it."

And it was all too much. The table, the tire swing, the horse riding…the man standing in the doorway holding her son. If she stayed, she'd never leave and that simply wasn't an option.

"I—I have to go."

She crossed the room, took Mason from Hayes's arms, but he didn't move out of her way to let her through.

"Why are you running?"

Keeping her eyes locked on the tire swing outside the back door, Alexa patted Mason's back and held him tight. "Because I can't do this. You don't need me to heal. You seem to be doing fine."

"I'm not," he muttered. "I want you here."

She shifted her focus to him, her eyes locking onto his. "But for how long?"

The muscle in his jaw tightened as silence settled heavy between them. His eyes darted to her mouth, but Alexa couldn't let him kiss her because she wanted so much more than a kiss.

She wanted to start thinking about a future and moving on, and no one had stirred anything within her like Hayes.

Yet she had to keep her son in the forefront of her thoughts. He needed stability in his life. Not only that, Alexa worried what would happen if Hayes decided family life wasn't for him. Sure, he was close to his own family, but she was a package deal. He had so many issues to deal with and adding that instant family to the mix hadn't been on his list.

Plus, she'd kept Scott's identity to herself. She'd thought they wouldn't see each other again so she hadn't brought it up when she'd been at Hayes's house. Now though, they were seeing each other and that secret hovered between them. Had she just told him when she realized it, maybe it wouldn't have been a big deal, but enough time had passed that he would feel betrayed by her silence once he found out.

There were just too many barriers between her and the man she wanted. But she was discovering over and over he was the one man she couldn't have.

Fourteen

Hayes's father wasn't looking any better and his mind was being flat-out cruel today. Hayes had visited earlier and was instantly confused for Nolan, but not Nolan now—the Nolan in kindergarten.

Having the most influential man in his life not even recognize him was hell on Hayes. But he couldn't stay away. No matter how far gone the patriarch was, Hayes had to see his dad, had to talk to him and use him as a sounding board. Now more than ever he wanted his father's advice, but that hadn't happened.

His dad had stared out the window and started talking about his wife in the present tense, as if she hadn't been gone for years. Then he'd turned his attention to Hayes and told him when he grew up, he should find someone to love and settle down and have babies to continue on at Pebblebrook. He went on and on about finding the love of his life, how he almost let her go once but came to his senses and put his pride aside.

Hayes knew all about how his parents had almost lost each other because of his father's pride. His mother had often reminded him in a joking manner.

Now that he was home, all he wanted to do was ride. He needed to talk to Colt, though. The engineer had been out early this morning and his survey had ended up on Hayes's property. Hell no. The dude ranch would come to fruition without infringing on his area. That was nonnegotiable.

He pulled up next to the stable and didn't see Colt, but that didn't mean anything. After several minutes of searching, Hayes gave up and started walking toward Colt's house. Finally, he found him in his study on the second floor behind a closed door.

"You hiding from the world?" Hayes asked, closing the door at his back.

Colt didn't even look up from the computer. "I'm working on this absurd marketing plan. I had it hired out and the damn thing came back looking like an amateur organized it. Annabelle gave me some ideas to fix it, but I'm actually looking for another firm. I don't want this messed up."

Hayes crossed the spacious room and took a seat in one of the leather club chairs across from his brother's desk. "I just came back from seeing Dad."

That got Colt's attention. "I was there yesterday. How was he today?"

Shaking his head, Hayes pulled off his hat and propped it on his knee. "He called me Nolan, referred to that time Nolan brought home a Mother's Day picture he'd made in kindergarten, then he fell into talking about Mom."

Colt eased back in his seat and sighed. "At least he's in a good mood when talking about Mom. I'll take that over the rage any day."

Hayes hadn't experienced those days with his father, but he'd heard that sometimes his father demanded to see his home, demanded someone take him to Pebblebrook. On those occasions, he still wasn't in his right mind. He was confused about where he was and why he wasn't home. Every day brought a different challenge.

"That's not why I came," Hayes stated. "I had a visit from the engineer. He mentioned expanding onto my property."

Colt eased forward, resting his forearms on the desk. "I never okayed that."

"Then why was he there?"

Colt shook his head. "He mentioned it to me in the beginning stages. He said there might be more revenue if we spread out over the land."

"And that was while I was away?" Hayes asked.

"Yeah. But Nolan and I had the area where we wanted the cabins marked off on the map." Colt narrowed his gaze. "What did he say to you? Because I'd hate to have to find another engineer this late in the game."

Hayes blew out a breath. "He was nosing more than anything, trying to get a feel from me what I thought. He left knowing exactly where I stand on outsiders on my part of the property."

The engineer wasn't the only reason Hayes was in a pissy mood. He was so damn confused about Alexa.

Tonight was the awards ceremony, which he hadn't mentioned to his family. He honestly didn't want this to be a big deal. If they found out later, fine. But if they knew now, they'd blow it all up and insist on attending.

He'd invited Alexa because he wanted to be with someone without feeling the pressure of being someone he wasn't. He wanted a friend.

But she was more than that, wasn't she? She was so much more and there was no denying he was in deep with her, which ultimately was going to put him in deep with Mason.

Damn it. That little boy was so sweet, so precious. He looked like Alexa and was so loving and free with his affection. When Hayes had been holding him... Even now just thinking about that weight in his arms had Hayes pausing, his heart tightening in fear...and affection.

Colt tipped his head. "Everything else okay?" he asked.

"Getting there." Hayes didn't know that he'd ever be the man he was before leaving, but he was slowly making steps to improve himself little by little. Alexa definitely had a hand in his recovery. "I need to head out."

Hayes came to his feet and slapped his hat back on his head. He had to get back to dress for the ceremony and leave with enough time to pick up Alexa and head to the governor's mansion, which was nearly two hours away.

"You know we're all here for you."

Hayes stilled in the doorway at Colt's words. He threw a glance over his shoulder. "Yeah. I know."

The look Colt gave him was that same one he'd had when Hayes had first returned. Pity. When would they stop? When would they start acting like he wasn't going to shatter?

Hayes headed back to his house. He had a date tonight. He hadn't spoken to Alexa since she'd left the ranch, but he knew she wouldn't go back on their date. Besides, he also knew she'd chosen a dress; she'd sent the others back. He'd paid for delivery of jewelry and shoes, too. Hopefully she'd found what she needed. He knew she'd be stunning in anything, but he wanted her to feel special.

There was too much going on in his mind for him to decipher the newfound emotions, but he didn't have time to figure them out. He wanted to get to Alexa and get this night over with.

As he pulled up to his house, he knew he'd be lying if he said he wasn't going to try to seduce her. He meant it when he said he wanted her still. Relationships weren't for him, but Alexa was the one bright spot in his life right now and he was damn well going to hold on to her…which meant he better wrap his mind around the fact he'd have to man up for Mason.

Hayes wasn't about to enter a child's life and not be anything less than stable.

Maybe she should've kept the classic black dress.

Alexa turned side to side in front of her floor-length mirror. The red dress draped over her shoulders and hugged her every curve…maybe a little too well. Something about the trumpet-style skirt and fitted bodice had made her feel sexy when she'd been trying on the host of dresses Hayes had sent.

But now that it was go time, she wondered if she should've ignored the sexy and kept the black with a modest scoop neck.

What did one wear to a governor's mansion?

Alexa smoothed a hand down her abdomen, hoping to rid herself of some of those nerves. Sadie had offered to take Mason for the night. All Alexa had to say was that she had a date and Sadie jumped at the opportunity to quiz Alexa. She didn't give in. What she and Hayes shared was… Honestly, she wasn't even sure, so how was she supposed to tell anyone else?

Just as she fastened the bracelet around her wrist, her doorbell rang. In that instant, her heart sped up and the chaos of jumbled nerves returned.

She headed toward the door figuring if she was nervous, she couldn't imagine what Hayes was feeling. The man didn't want to leave his ranch, let alone go to some fancy ceremony where he was going to be awarded for something he felt guilty about.

Alexa wasn't sure what had happened overseas, but those events had changed Hayes forever.

Pulling in a shaky breath, she opened her door…and was greeted with the sexiest man she'd ever seen. He'd forgone the cowboy hat and boots, the well-worn jeans and T-shirt. He stood before her wearing his uniform. The black single-breasted jacket stretched across his broad shoulders. Various pins and patches adorned the shoulders and chest. The offset beret seemed to draw even more attention to those black eyes.

The man flawlessly slid from hardworking rancher to hero in uniform.

Alexa shivered at the way he raked his eyes over her. Slowly, inch by inch, as if assessing what she wore beneath. Arousal curled through her, as she knew it would. She hadn't seen him in days and just being near him put her body on high alert. She hadn't mentally prepared herself for the uniform, though.

"We're ditching the ceremony," he growled as he stepped over the threshold. He slid his arms around her waist and aligned his body with hers. "Damn, Alexa."

She held on to his biceps to keep her balance. "We can't ditch. I'm pretty sure there's some unwritten law about snubbing the governor, especially considering you're the guest of honor."

"You smell so damn good," he murmured against her ear.

Alexa shivered against him and was having a difficult time recalling why they couldn't just stay here.

Oh, yeah. The award and the fact she'd promised herself not to get more deeply involved. Because if she took things further, then she'd have to tell him who her husband was. And because she was still unsure about bringing a man into Mason's life. She didn't want to confuse her son. She made continual efforts to make sure his life was secure.

"We're going to be late if we don't go."

Hayes eased back. "You're the perfect reason to be late and they'd all understand once they saw you in this dress."

Apparently she'd kept the right one.

"Thanks for this," she told him, stepping back and removing herself from his arms. She couldn't think when he touched her. "I would've gotten my own dress, though."

"I wanted to buy this for you."

"And the jewelry and shoes?" she questioned. "I thought I was just borrowing these things."

"They're yours," he replied, tugging at the cuffs of his jacket. "You could've kept everything I sent."

Alexa laughed. "There were nearly thirty dresses to choose from."

He stared back as if he didn't see the problem. First of all, what would a single mom and preschool teacher do with that many formal dresses? Second, she couldn't even imagine the cost. This dress alone was probably one paycheck. She'd seen the label and that wasn't even adding in the cost of her accessories.

Yeah, definitely nothing she could wear to the playground with Mason.

"Thanks for not backing out," he told her, all joking and flirting set aside.

"I wouldn't do that to you."

Hayes nodded and held her attention with those serious black eyes. "I know you wouldn't. You should have, but you didn't. Let's just put all our issues aside and enjoy our night together."

She opened her mouth, but he held up a hand. "I know it's selfish," he went on. "If you want to talk, I'll listen, but after the ceremony."

Alexa stepped forward and framed his clean-shaven face. "I know this is difficult for you, but you are deserving."

He started to turn his face away, but she pulled him back. "You are."

A corner of his mouth kicked up. "Are you wearing underwear?"

Alexa smacked his chest, getting a palm-full of medals. "We better go."

"It would help distract me from the award I don't want if you just tell me what you're wearing underneath." He snaked a hand out and ran it over her backside. Letting out a groan, he muttered, "A thong. You're killing me."

Alexa shifted away from him, knowing full well if they didn't get out that door, they'd be in her bedroom… if they even made it that far.

"Now that you have something else to concentrate on, let's go." She grabbed her clutch and placed her keys and phone inside before closing the gold clasp. "I hope they have chocolate cake at this dinner."

Hayes held the door open for her and swatted her on the butt. "Dessert isn't happening at the ceremony."

Shivers raced through her as she came to the realization that they would end up back here. And the realization that he was going to keep coming around and she was going to let him.

She was going to have to tell him the truth about Scott and then he'd have to trust that she never purposely betrayed him.

But not tonight.

Tonight was about him getting a prestigious award whether he wanted to accept it or not. Tomorrow, she would tell him everything.

Tomorrow, she would explain how she'd fallen for him and see if this could be more than just a friendship with intimacy.

For the first time in two years, Alexa was ready to move on and cling to the happiness she'd discovered. If only her lie by omission didn't stand in the way... If only Hayes wanted a family, because she and Mason were a team.

Fifteen

The handshaking, fake smiles, impromptu speech and that damn shiny award with his name engraved on the gold plate were all sickening.

Hayes drove back toward Alexa's home. It was close to midnight according to the glow from the dash clock. Alexa had slipped her shoes off onto the floorboard of his sporty car. He'd opted for something nicer than his truck, mostly for Alexa because he didn't give a damn what anyone else thought of him.

She hadn't said a word since they left. It was almost as if she knew he needed to be alone inside his mind. That was what was so great about her. She just knew what he needed.

"Seven of my best friends were killed that day." He wound through the streets leading to her town house. He didn't even realize he'd started speaking, but now that he'd started, he found he didn't want to stop. "We were sent in to rescue three women and eighteen girls at a school that had been overtaken. We had a solid plan, but nothing is foolproof."

Alexa reached across, sliding her hand over his on the console. Silence settled between them, but her act of compassion spoke volumes. Damn it. She was getting to him. He'd known she was, had known the more he was with her the more likely he was to want more of her.

"I'll spare you the details, but there was an ambush," he added, trying in vain to block the images that played like a horror movie inside his head. "The women and girls were saved, I was spared, but…"

"I won't tell you not to have survivor's guilt." Her soft words filled the cramped area. "That's human nature to wonder what if. I went through it. I'm still going through it. I wonder what would've happened had we known about my husband's condition. Could we have prevented his death? But I can't get stuck in that mindset, mostly because of Mason. He deserves to have his mother at one hundred percent."

"Mason is a lucky boy," Hayes stated. "I'm sure he'll know how loved he is."

Alexa sighed. "That's my hope. But you're doing remarkably well, considering. You only tensed a few times tonight being with all those people."

He turned his hand over, lacing his fingers with hers. "Figures you'd notice."

"I know you," she said simply.

Wasn't that the truth. After such a short time, she'd honed right in on what made him tick, what his fears were, how to handle them. He hadn't wanted to show any vulnerability, but Alexa never made him feel as if he had. She made him feel…human. Like everything he was going through was okay and he'd make it.

"I just pictured your underwear."

Her laughter warmed him, taking him to that place that was so perfect, so right. He hadn't thought such a place existed after he'd come home, but since meeting Alexa, he'd discovered maybe there was a bright spot in the world. Maybe that was the one thing he shouldn't fear.

"I could tell when you'd look at me across the room," she told him. "I knew exactly what you were thinking."

"Good. Because I'm about to show you exactly what was running through my mind."

He pulled into her drive and barely got the car in park before he reached across and cupped the back of her head, bringing her mouth to his.

Finally. He hadn't kissed her all evening, hadn't touched her in the way he'd wanted to. In short, he'd been on his best behavior.

Now, he was about to be on his worst. He reached for the zipper on the back of the dress. "How the hell did you get into this thing?" he growled against her lips.

Alexa laughed, her eyes shining bright as she stared back at him. "Side zipper, but we better get inside before my neighbors see us making out like teenagers."

"Your neighbors' lights are off."

Alexa tugged on the door handle. "I'm not taking the chance."

Hayes followed her inside. They barely made it in the door before he backed her up against it, flicked the lock and caged her head between his forearms.

"You have three seconds to get that side zipper or I'm going to rip this dress off."

Her hands were moving as she tossed her head back with a sultry laugh. "You paid for it."

"Best money I've ever spent."

As the dress peeled away and fell below her breasts,

Hayes was on her. He couldn't get enough and this entire evening of foreplay had nearly done him in. Watching her curves move beneath that red dress, the way her dark hair flowed around her shoulders, seeing her laugh across the room, then catch his eye. He knew he wasn't the only one thinking of this.

Her little striptease had him jerking his uniform off, quickly ridding himself of everything so he could be skin to skin. They still hadn't turned on lights, but he didn't need them. There wasn't a spot on her body he wasn't familiar with.

He lifted her against the door, dipping his head to capture her mouth once again. Alexa's legs locked around his waist and he wasted no time in joining their bodies. Finesse would come later—much later. Right now he had a need that had been building all night.

Her fingers dug into his shoulders as she arched that sweet body against his. Hayes slid a hand down the dip in her waist and over the flare of her hip, gripping her to hold her in place. She dug her heels into his backside and Hayes knew she was on the brink.

He tore his lips from hers and shifted just enough to see her face. The slight glow from the porch light filtered in through the window, slashing just enough of a beam across her face for him to fully appreciate her pleasure.

"Look at me," he commanded, squeezing her hip.

Those black eyes immediately locked onto his and a second later she cried out. That's exactly what he'd been waiting on. Seeing her come apart in his arms, knowing he was the one who made her lose control was all he wanted. Her hips quickened as she came apart and that's all it took to have him joining her.

Hayes's body trembled as he fisted one hand on the

door beside her head and continued to hold on to her hip. His knee was starting to shake from being too weak, but hell if he'd give in now.

Alexa ran her fingertips up and down his back, his arms, murmuring something in Spanish as he came down from the tremors. Resting his forehead against hers, he pulled in a breath of sweet jasmine…the same scent she'd tortured him with all night.

"Do you have the energy to get to the bedroom?" she asked.

Hayes laughed. "If it's not far. Or we could sleep here on the floor."

"Let me down," she told him, untangling her legs from his waist. "Your knee has to be hurting."

He stepped back and said nothing.

"Exactly," she confirmed. "You shifted too much and kept fisting your hand by my head. Get in bed and rest that."

Hayes instantly lifted her up and over his shoulder.

"Put me down," she cried, smacking his back. "Hayes, your leg is going to give out and we'll both be down."

"Like hell," he growled. "I'll rest it when we get in there. Better yet, you can give me a rubdown. Now tell me where the bedroom is."

"Last door on the right."

He palmed her backside, earning him another laugh from her. Damn, that laugh made everything seem so right, so perfect. Could such happiness be his for the taking? Alexa had lost her husband and never claimed to be looking for a relationship. Hell, he hadn't either, but the idea of letting her go, the thought of another man even touching her settled a new level of rage within him.

She also hadn't mentioned wanting or even needing a man to fill the role of daddy to her son. Maybe that's not something she wanted at all. It was one thing to be involved in an affair, but quite another to become a family.

Hayes's eyes had gotten used to the darkness and the small night-light glowing from Mason's bedroom across the hall lit up enough for him to make out the shape of her bed. Hayes dropped her on the end and instantly was on her.

"I'll take that rubdown in a bit," he told her as he covered her body with his. "First I'm going to show you exactly how thankful I am that you went with me tonight."

Alexa stretched, smiling when her body protested. She was sore in the most glorious ways. The sun shone through the sheers of her room and one thick arm draped across her midsection. How could she not wake up with a smile on her face after last night?

She was glad she'd let Mason stay over with Sadie. Alexa knew they'd get home late and didn't want to put Sadie out too much…or more than she already was. But Sadie was so happy that Alexa was going on a date, she'd eagerly volunteered to watch Mason all night.

Hayes shifted and groaned, and his heavy leg slid over hers. The coarse hairs made her shiver. Who knew all the little things she missed from a man's touch? Obviously, he was the first man in this bed since Scott… but Alexa didn't feel like this was wrong in any way.

That's how she knew it was time to come clean about who her husband was.

She flattened her hand over Hayes's arm and slid it up and over his shoulder. Keeping her eyes on his face, she watched as his lids fluttered. His hold on her tightened as he pulled her closer.

"Stop, temptress," he mumbled.

Alexa couldn't help but laugh. "You slept good."

"I'd keep sleeping if you weren't feeling me up."

Shifting in his arms, Alexa nipped at his chin. "I believe I woke with your bare arm over my midsection and then you wrapped your leg around me. You want to be felt up."

Hayes slid his hand over her bare hip and settled on the dip in her waist. Alexa's body instantly responded, but then he curled those fingers in and started tickling her.

"Hayes," she squealed. "Stop that."

A cell started ringing somewhere in the house. She didn't recognize the tone, so it must be his. She smacked at his arms as he continued to tickle her. He wrestled her beneath him as she continued to wriggle around and try to dodge the torture.

"Your cell," she panted, trying to breathe. "It's… Stop that. It's ringing."

Hayes loomed over her, the widest smile on his face. She hadn't seen him like that before. A smirk here and there, a naughty grin, sure. But a full-fledged genuine smile was staring back at her. Alexa's heart tumbled over in her chest.

"What's that look for?" he asked, resting his hands on either side of her head. "You were just laughing and now you look on the verge of tears."

The cell stopped in the other room, silence once again settling around them.

"I haven't been this happy in a long time." She reached up, framed his face and stared into his eyes. "I didn't think I could be, but you've done something to me. I wasn't expecting this."

"I—"

His cell went off again. With a sigh, he eased off her and turned to head from the room. He'd only taken two steps when he froze. His shoulders tensed and Alexa followed his line of vision.

Her heart immediately sank. How could she have forgotten about that photo? The wedding picture of her and Scott had sat so long on her dresser, and she hadn't been able to remove it after his death. Then she just…didn't.

The cell continued to ring, the only thing breaking through the heavy tension. Hayes slowly made his way to the silver frame and picked it up. Alexa sat up in the bed, pulling the comforter up and under her arms.

"Were you ever going to tell me?" he asked.

Alexa closed her eyes, not wanting to see his face when he turned around. She was a coward—clearly.

"I didn't know at first," she said. "Then I didn't think we'd see each other anymore."

When he didn't say anything, Alexa risked looking up, but wished she hadn't. Hayes stood at the end of her bed, clutching the picture in one hand and staring at her as if he hadn't just been with her all night, as if everything up until this point had been a lie.

"What's your excuse for all the times you've seen me since then?" he asked.

"I have no excuse," she muttered, picking at the thread on the comforter. "I was going to tell you, but I didn't know how. When you first mentioned his name, I was so shocked. Then I knew what we had was temporary so I figured I would keep it to myself and not make things awkward. Plus, talking about Scott with you seemed wrong, like if I started opening up about him too much it would seem like I was ready to move on and I didn't know if I was."

The muscle ticked in his jaw. The cell stopped, then started seconds later, and finally stopped again.

"Then when you showed up at my house and we

fell back into…well, us, I didn't know what to say. I hadn't expected to see you again and I was afraid if I said anything you'd see it as betrayal. There was no good time, Hayes."

She wanted him to look at her so she could see his eyes, to hopefully get a glimpse of what he was thinking, feeling.

"I didn't want you hurt any more," she whispered. "I care for you. You have to know that."

Hayes cursed and sat the picture at the end of the bed. He stared at it a moment before raking a hand through his messy hair.

He turned without looking at her and stormed from her room. Alexa climbed out of bed and quickly pulled on a T-shirt and panties. As she headed down the hall, she saw Hayes holding the cell between his ear and his shoulder. He hopped from one foot to the other pulling on his pants.

"I'll be there in five minutes."

He shoved the cell in his pants pocket, grabbed his jacket and shoes without putting them on.

"My father had a stroke," he told her without looking her way.

Alexa stepped forward. "I'll drive—"

"No." That sharp gaze of his cut to her. "You're getting your wish. We don't have to see each other anymore and then you won't have to worry about telling me any more truths you conveniently forgot."

Her heart broke, shattered. "Hayes."

He jerked on the door and stepped out, not bothering to spare her one last glance. The door didn't slam, but the final click resonated throughout the open space.

Wrapping her arms around her midsection, Alexa stared at the door. He was gone. She'd done this. Had he not seen that picture, had she told him the minute she realized who his best friend had been, she would probably be with him now.

Who would be there for him? How bad off was his father? Alexa knew how much his family meant to him and knew how fragile his father's health had been.

How would Hayes cope? With all the ugliness he'd experienced, Alexa prayed he wouldn't lose his father.

She padded back to the bedroom, stopping just inside the bedroom door to look at the messed-up bed and the image of her and Scott on their wedding day.

It didn't matter that he'd told her he didn't want to see her again; she had to explain herself. Not that she had much defense, but she had to go to him. She couldn't let him believe she'd set out on betrayal. Plus, she needed to check on him regarding his father.

Tonight, she'd go to him and pray she hadn't lost this second chance she'd been given. How often did anyone get another shot at love? She'd been so afraid before, too scared to even think about opening her heart, but not anymore. Hayes had taught her all about courage and just how strong she was.

To think she'd been worried about having a man in Mason's life. There was no better man to fill the role of father to her sweet son. Hayes might be afraid, but she wasn't going to let him hide and she wasn't going to let him think for a second that she'd hurt him on purpose.

She would make him see that she loved him, that they belonged together…that they were a family.

Sixteen

"He's going to be all right."

Hayes had barely gotten into the waiting room when Piper, Nolan's wife, delivered the news.

"The doctor said the damage is minor from what they can tell, but they are keeping him."

Hayes breathed easily for what felt like the first time in an hour. Between the news of his father and Alexa...

No. He couldn't think of her. Not here when he was surrounded by his family.

"Why are you in uniform?"

Hayes turned at Colt's voice. "I didn't go home last night," Hayes explained.

"And you were out somewhere that required a uniform?"

Colt crossed his arms over his chest as Nolan came up behind him wearing his scrubs. Most likely his brother had been on call when they'd brought their father in.

"I had a ceremony I had to attend." They didn't need to know any more. He'd tell them about the award later, but right now they had more pressing matters. "What's going on with Dad?"

"He was slurring his speech with the nurse at the assisted living facility and had some paralysis on his right side," Nolan explained. "She called the squad to bring him in and they ran some tests, did an ultrasound of his carotid. It's a minor stroke and we won't know more until the days progress, but he's going to be all right."

How was any of this all right? His father suffered from dementia and now he'd had a minor stroke? Hayes felt like the only stable world he'd known was crumbling around him.

"Can I see him?"

Nolan nodded. "He's not supposed to have visitors, but I requested an exception. Only a couple minutes. Room 108. It's at the end of the hall."

Hayes nodded and started to push past his brothers. Colt reached out and gripped Hayes's arm.

"After this, we want to know what you were doing," he murmured, probably so the ladies couldn't hear. "You wanted so far away from the Army, to forget what happened, and you show up in uniform after a ceremony? Something isn't jibing."

Hayes jerked his arm away and continued down the hall toward his father's room. He stopped just outside the door, pulling in a deep breath and trying to prepare himself for what he might see.

As he rounded the corner, Hayes zeroed in on his frail father lying in the bed, his head turned away. His thinning, silver hair had been smoothed back. There was once a time this man never went without his black hat. He'd been robust, strong, the rock of their entire family. Now that duty fell to the four boys…well, three when they removed Beau from the equation.

Hayes needed to make sure someone contacted Beau just as soon as he was done here.

As Hayes moved closer, his father shifted and turned his way. A ghost of a smile slid across his lips.

"Hey, Dad."

"Hayes."

Relief like he'd never known crashed through him. "You remember me."

"For now." His father's eyes filled with tears. "I'm sorry, son. I—I hate the b-burden I've become."

Hayes eased a hip on the edge of the bed and took his father's worn hand. "You're not a burden. You're our father and we'll do anything for you."

"I raised good b-boys," he stuttered, then narrowed his gaze. "U-uniform?"

"Long story," Hayes stated, then found that he wanted to share it. He wanted to have a moment with his father because it might be the last. "I got an award last night. I was invited to the governor's mansion to receive it."

"That's a-amazing. S-so proud…of you. Did your brothers g-go?"

Hayes shook his head and glanced to his father's frail hand in his. "No. I didn't tell them. I ended up taking a date."

"Someone serious?"

"I thought she was," Hayes admitted. "Not sure anymore."

"Since last n-night?" his father questioned. "If you think…she is, d-don't let her go."

Hayes glanced back to his father. "Neither of us were looking for a relationship."

His father attempted a smile and squeezed his hand.

"Those are the best k-kind. Your mother and I w-weren't, either. L-loved her more than anything. S-still do."

Hayes didn't want to think about this right now. He didn't want to try to deal with Alexa and her reasons for keeping something so monumental from him while he was also worried about his father's health.

He understood that she'd been stunned when he'd mentioned Scott's name. That was understandable, but she'd had ample time to come to terms with the fact. She should've trusted what they had. She should've trusted him enough to tell him the truth.

He hadn't just gotten involved with her, he'd gotten involved with Mason and thinking of both of them out of his life had a void settling deep in his heart.

"I should go and let you rest." But he didn't want to end this moment. Would his father even know who he was next time? "I love you, Dad."

"Love you, Hayes."

After placing a kiss on his father's forehead, Hayes forced himself to leave the room. If that was the last time he heard his father say he loved him and call him by name, that would be enough. Hayes honestly hadn't believed he'd get that again. Perhaps the uniform helped his father recognize him or perhaps his father just knew that at this moment Hayes needed him now more than ever.

No matter the reasons, Hayes was thankful to have had those few minutes. He needed to check to see if anyone had contacted Beau and then he wanted to head home. There was too much swirling around his mind and he just wanted to be left alone.

Alone.

Ironic that was exactly what he'd wanted when he

came home, but then he'd been enveloped by his brothers, their wives, their kids... Alexa and Mason.

The pain she'd left buried inside him wasn't going away anytime soon. He knew she'd come to him, knew she'd want to defend herself. So he needed time to prepare his heart. Because as hard as he tried, his damn heart had gone and gotten involved. Now he had to figure out how the hell he was going to move on.

Maybe he should've saved some demo work because Hayes could sure have done some damage with the sledgehammer. Unfortunately, he was on the back end of the kitchen renovation and coming close to the finish.

In the past several days he'd gotten his cabinets installed. Countertops, backsplash and new appliances were to be installed next week. Now he was working on the lighting over the giant table that mocked him. He couldn't look at the damn thing without seeing Alexa and her expression when she saw it.

For the last two nights he'd slept like hell and had pretty much kept to himself. He'd visited his father a couple times, but he'd reverted back inside his mind. Hayes knew he would, but there was still that sliver of hope each time he went that maybe there would be some remembrance.

When the back door opened, Hayes steeled himself for the slam. He turned just as the screen door hit and Nolan and Colt were standing there like a force...one he didn't want to deal with right now.

"This must be important to get you both here at the same time."

Nolan stepped in and glanced around. "You've done a lot with the place since I was here last."

Hayes went back to screwing in the base for the light over the table. "That's the goal."

"Where were you the other night?" Colt demanded.

Hayes twisted the nut around the screw and grunted. "Well, Dad, I don't have to tell you everything I do."

Glancing down onto the table, Hayes searched for the screwdriver to tighten the rest of the screws.

"We just want to help," Nolan stated, handing him the tool. "You haven't mentioned one thing about the Army in months, so you have to understand that when you show up looking like you slept in your uniform, we get a little concerned."

Concentrating on the light, Hayes let the silence stretch out. Once he was done, he climbed down and pulled in a breath.

"I was at the governor's mansion receiving an award."

"What the hell?" Colt shouted.

"And you didn't tell us before now?" Nolan demanded at the same time.

Hayes shrugged. "I didn't want you guys to make a big deal about it."

"A big deal?" Colt questioned. "You're joking, right? This is a very big deal."

"I didn't want the award." He still didn't want it. "Taking that seems so wrong, like I'm actually accepting the fact that all of those deaths happened, like I'm moving on with my life when they can't move on with theirs."

A weight settled heavy on his chest. Isn't that what happened with Alexa? She'd been afraid to mention Scott because that would've brought to life the fact that she was moving on and she hadn't been ready. His response to receiving that award was the exact same thing.

He hadn't wanted to come to grips with the fact he was moving on.

Hayes cleared his throat, pushing aside the turmoil of regret. "The award was given to the wrong man anyway."

"If the governor gave it to you, then that was the right man." Colt crossed the room and stood on the other side of the table, his hands propped on his hips. "Why the hell didn't you want us to know? Because we might care? Because we might want to go and show support?"

"Do you think Annabelle and Piper are going to enjoy hearing that you didn't want them there?" Nolan added, twisting the knife deeper.

Hayes knew this would be their reaction, but he hadn't thought about his sisters-in-law. "I'll explain the same thing to them. I didn't want a big fuss made."

"Too damn bad," Colt gritted out. "Why do you think we want to cause a fuss? Because we're damn glad you came home, Hayes. Maybe we want to celebrate the fact you're alive."

Hayes turned away. "Well, maybe I'm not quite ready for that yet."

He went to the box with the antique light fixture and stared down at it. His first thought when he'd seen it was Alexa. Would she approve? She'd had so many ideas for the house, specifically this kitchen.

"So you went to this awards ceremony alone and decided to keep everyone else at arm's length?" Nolan asked.

Hayes glanced over his shoulder. "I didn't go alone."

Colt's eyes narrowed. "Alexa."

"Where is she now?" Nolan asked. "She wasn't at the hospital with you. She's not here, but she's serious enough to take to the governor's mansion."

She had been important enough to take. She'd been…
everything.

That couldn't be right, could it? Alexa had been
someone he'd turned to when he needed an outsider who
wasn't offering pity. Yes, his heart had gotten wrestled
into the mix, but he'd been confused and beaten down.
It was only natural. Right?

"We're…not together," he confirmed.

Colt let out a bark of laughter and adjusted his hat.
"So you pushed her away, too?"

"No, asshole, if you have to know, I found out she'd
been married to Scott."

Nolan's brows shot up. "That's Scott's widow?"

Hayes nodded. "I just found out the morning I got
the call about Dad. I didn't leave her house on the best
of terms."

"And you've not reached out since?" Colt guessed.

Hayes turned and sank down on the bench that ran
along one side of the table. "Just leave me alone."

He was done. Exhausted. The lack of sleep, the ache
in his heart, he just wanted to get through this on his
own…like everything else.

"Being alone doesn't seem to be working for you."
Nolan slid in next to him. "I'm not trying to get into
your love life—"

"Then don't."

"But you seemed almost happy when Alexa was
here," Nolan went on.

"How the hell would you know?"

Colt eased onto the bench on the other side. "Because
I saw you. Annabelle saw you. You think we all don't
talk? There was something so different about you. You
actually smiled."

"I smile now."

Okay, that sounded like a lame argument. But he smiled...didn't he?

"Is it because she has a baby?" Nolan asked. "I know you're worried about moving on with your life, about getting involved with people again, so I'm sure kids are scary."

He didn't want to discuss Mason with his brothers. He sure as hell wasn't ready to have the family bonding talk about how to raise kids and how to form a life and step into the role of dad.

"I know your fiancée did a number on you and that was on top of whatever hell you experienced during that extraction." Nolan shifted and kept his focus on Hayes. "But are you really going to blame Alexa for being married to your friend and not telling you? Hell, you've kept nearly everything from us and we still love you."

"I don't love her."

Colt snorted. "I didn't love Annabelle, either. And then I realized I couldn't live without her or her girls."

Hayes could live without Alexa and Mason. He could, damn it.

He just didn't want to. He wanted them both, he wanted them to be his family and he wanted to provide for them, to take away their worries and fears.

"Did you tell her about what happened over there?" Nolan asked.

Hayes nodded.

"Don't you think that speaks volumes, little brother? She knows and you've yet to open up to your own family."

There was no hurt in Nolan's tone, just a matter-of-fact manner.

"Damn it," he muttered, dropping his head into his hands. "I'll talk to you guys. Just not yet, okay?"

Nolan's hand came down hard on Hayes's back. "If she was important enough to take to the ceremony and to tell your darkest secrets to, don't you think she's important enough to apologize to?"

"I didn't do anything wrong."

He glanced across to Colt who merely raised a brow.

"Fine, I left without hearing her side, but Dad was in the hospital. And since then… I just needed to get my head on straight."

"If you wait too long she might not want to explain at all," Nolan stated.

His brothers came to their feet and headed to the door.

"What? That's it?" Hayes asked. "You two have some code? When I'm emotionally beaten down you get up and leave?"

"Pretty much," Colt confirmed as he adjusted his hat again. "But we didn't discuss it."

Hayes rested his hands on the table and pushed up. "Get the hell out of here. I have more work to do."

"You also have to call Annabelle and Piper and tell them about your award," Colt stated. "And when they want to throw you a party or a dinner, or any other celebration, you'll let them and you'll be thankful."

Hayes saluted. "Yes, sir."

They left with a slam of the back door that had Hayes jumping, but at least he was still upright and not in the fetal position on the floor.

He had a few finishing touches to do before contacting Alexa. He wanted things to be perfect, but he also wanted an explanation. She'd hurt him, that he couldn't overlook. But he would give her a chance to defend herself because she deserved it…and he missed her.

Seventeen

Alexa smoothed a hand down her dress and knocked on Hayes's back door. She seriously should've called, but she didn't want him to flat-out tell her no. She figured if she was there in person, maybe he'd listen to her. She couldn't wait another day. Two had seemed like a lifetime and she was taking a risk driving here and crossing through Elliott land like she owned the place.

Shifting Mason higher on her hip, she stepped back and waited for Hayes to answer the door. Mason had fallen asleep on the way over and was still out. He rested his little head on her shoulder and she drew her strength from him.

Even when this was all said and done, even if she left here with her heart broken, she still had her amazing son and he was the greatest thing in her life.

The wood door swung open, leaving the screen separating them. Hayes had on his jeans and a large buckle with the Pebblebrook emblem, but no shirt.

When he said nothing, Alexa cleared her throat. "I hope you're not in the middle of anything. I just... I wanted to talk to you."

Hayes reached out, pushing the screen door open. Without a word, he gestured her inside. Well, at least that was something. He didn't close the door in her face and didn't tell her no.

"Oh, my word, Hayes." She glanced around the room, taking in all the clean lines, the bold splashes of color. The table now had benches, the appliances were missing, but everything else was absolutely perfect. "This is even better than I imagined it would be."

He crossed to the table and started cleaning up some tools. "I just got this light hung," he told her as he moved the large box back toward the laundry room. He sat the tools in the toolbox on the floor and turned back to her. "Say whatever it is you have to say."

Okay, so he wasn't going to make this easy. She hadn't expected him to and she probably didn't deserve the break.

"I know saying sorry now seems convenient and the easy way to start, but I am sorry."

Mason shifted in her arms, but she patted his back and he settled.

"Sit down," Hayes demanded. "You don't need to be standing and holding him. He's got to be heavy."

Alexa smiled. "I'm used to him and I doubt I'll be here long."

She'd say what she needed to say and leave. The ball would be in his court, so to speak.

"I had no clue you were Scott's friend," she started. "I knew he had a best friend in school he called Cowboy. He told me his friend went into the Army and I knew you guys texted and talked on occasion. But I swear, I never heard him say your real name. I never really asked, either."

Hayes remained across the room. He crossed his arms over that broad chest and continued to stare at her with that darkened gaze. Alexa laced her fingers beneath Mason's bottom and kept going.

"I didn't know anything until I mentioned the movie and you said his name," she admitted. "And by then we'd slept together. I figured once I left, we'd never see each other again and you wouldn't have to know. You were so angry with your fiancée and your commanding officer, I just didn't want you to see similarities. Admitting everything would've meant I was feeling something for you and that I was accepting that my original family was in the past. I realize that was a mistake, but I did what I thought was right. I was afraid.

"But then you came to my house," she went on as she paced the room. "I thought staying away from you would be best, but you came by and I had no willpower. The more time I spent with you, the more my feelings were growing and I never thought I'd have feelings for another man again."

"And what do you feel?" he asked.

Alexa stilled, then turned back around. "I fell in love with you. I'm completely in love with you, and so is Mason."

If he was shocked at her words, he didn't show it. This was one of those times she wished her blunt mouth would zip it, but she was here to tell him the whole truth so she couldn't stop now.

"I have no idea when I fell for you," she went on, ignoring her nerves. She'd come this far. "But I knew you needed to know who I was, who my husband was."

"Why the different last names?" he asked.

Alexa shrugged. "I never changed my name when we married. I just wanted to keep mine."

Hayes dropped his arms and crossed the room. Her eyes darted to that bare chest, the smattering of dark hair, the swirling ink. He was a beautiful man inside and out and it absolutely hurt to know she might have destroyed their chance.

"Do you want to say anything else?" he asked, looming over her.

Alexa swallowed. "No. I just want you to know I'm sorry I hurt you."

Damn it. Her throat was burning. Tears were on the horizon and she wanted to at least get back to her car before she lost it.

Mason stirred again, this time lifting his head and glancing around. He rubbed his eyes and dropped his head back onto her shoulder then toyed with the strands of her hair. She knew he was awake—all the more reason to leave.

When Hayes continued to stare and the silence became too much, Alexa turned and headed for the door. There was nothing else she could do.

"Stay."

His command cut through the tension. Alexa didn't turn around as she clutched Mason tighter.

"I listened to you, so now you'll listen to me."

Alexa swallowed and eased around to face him. Hayes crossed the room, his limp a little more prominent today, most likely from the renovating he'd been doing.

When he reached for Mason, Alexa started to protest, but her son instantly wrapped his arms around Hayes's neck. The sight was too much to bear. The strong cowboy she'd fallen for holding her fatherless son…she'd hit her breaking point.

The tears fell without control and Alexa covered her face—both to block the touching sight and to hide the fact she was a wreck.

"Don't cry," he told her. "I haven't even told you I love you yet."

Alexa froze, slowly dropping her hands. There was no way she'd heard him right, but when she met his gaze, he was smiling. Hayes Elliott held her son and was smiling like she'd never seen before.

"I was coming for you," he told her as he closed the narrow space between them. "I wanted to finish working in here, maybe grab a shower, but I was coming for you. I didn't give you a chance to talk before and I wanted to believe you didn't betray me."

"I did betray you by not telling you the second I knew," she whispered, swiping at her damp cheeks.

"You didn't betray me," he told her. "You guarded yourself from more hurt and you didn't want to hurt me in the process. If the roles were reversed, I can't say I wouldn't have done the same. Actually, I have done this, so I get where you're coming from."

Hope spread through her, warming her and healing her shattered heart. "Can we get back to the part where you said you love me? Because if you love me, does that mean you forgive me?"

With one strong arm around Mason, Hayes reached for her with his other and pulled her in tight. "You're everything, Alexa. When I said stay, I meant forever. And you will be taking my name. I'd like to adopt Mason as my own, but only if you want him to have the Elliott name. I understand if you—"

She placed her finger over his lips. "I want both of us to have your name."

He blew out a breath, grabbing her hand and kissing her fingertip. "It can't happen soon enough."

Unable to stop the flood of emotions, Alexa dropped her forehead to his shoulder and let the tears fall. She didn't care at this point. The relief, the happiness, the fact she was home with her son and the man she'd fallen so hard, so fast for, was just too much to take in.

"Tell me again." She lifted her head and wrapped her arms around Mason and Hayes. "Tell me you love me, because I can't get used to hearing that enough. I thought I'd leave here and never see you again."

His hand settled on her backside as he drew her closer. "This is home, Alexa. I want to build a life here, build a family."

The gasp escaped before she could stop herself. "You want more kids?"

With a slight shrug, he glanced to Mason who was wide-eyed and staring at his crying mother. "I'm not opposed to more. I love this little guy. I'm messed up, so I understand if you don't—"

Alexa put her finger over his lips. "Don't finish that sentence. If you want kids, I'll give them to you."

Hayes kissed her, hard, fast, then eased back. "What are the odds he's ready for bed? Because we could start practicing now."

"Oh, it will be a while before he goes to bed. He slept on the way over here. Maybe if we play outside or take him for a ride he can go to bed early."

Hayes curled his fingers into her rear end, pulling the fabric of the dress up. "Then you're mine," he growled against her lips.

"Yours."

"Forever."

Alexa hugged her family tighter. "Forever."

Epilogue

There was a party and he hadn't been invited.

What did Beau Elliott expect? He'd been gone from Pebblebrook for years. Busy making his life in Hollywood and living up to all the media claimed him to be. Playboy, throwing money around, billion-dollar home, traveling with a new woman each week.

Yeah, he'd been busy according to the press. But there was so much they didn't know.

Beau sat in his car halfway up the drive on the Pebblebrook ranch. There were kids playing in the front yard of Colt's house. Kids. His brothers had married and had kids.

Glancing in the rearview mirror, Beau swallowed the lump of fear, remorse.

What was he doing back here? What the hell did he expect to accomplish? His brothers would give him hell, and he deserved nothing less.

His father had had a stroke a week ago, but Beau hadn't been able to get away. He'd called the hospital every single day asking for updates. He'd also asked for his calls to be kept from his family.

Beau was dealing with some issues that couldn't be ignored or put aside. Not even his money could get him out of this.

Squeals of laughter came through his open windows. He watched as his brothers interacted with their wives or girlfriends…whatever the status was. He saw four children and wondered just how much had changed since he'd been gone.

He wasn't naive. Beau knew his family wouldn't exactly welcome him with open arms, but he had nowhere else to go. Oh, he had a flat in London and a cottage in Versailles, but he couldn't go to either of those places.

No matter where he'd been in his life, no matter what he'd been doing, he couldn't deny that Pebblebrook was home. And now more than ever, he needed to be here.

Beau put the car in Drive and started easing toward the entry just as he heard a cry from the infant in the back seat. His heart clenched.

Yeah, now more than ever he needed his family, his home.

* * * * *

*If you liked Hayes's story, don't miss
his brothers' romances in*
THE RANCHER'S HEIRS *series from
Jules Bennett!*

*TWIN SECRETS
CLAIMED BY THE RANCHER*

And pick up these other novels from Jules Bennett

*TRAPPED WITH THE TYCOON
FROM FRIEND TO FAKE FIANCÉ
HOLIDAY BABY SCANDAL*

Available now from Harlequin Desire!

***

And don't miss the next
BILLIONAIRES AND BABIES *story*
FOR THE SAKE OF HIS HEIR

*By Joanne Rock
Available February 2018!*

***

*If you're on Twitter, tell us what you think of
Harlequin Desire! #harlequindesire*

MILLS & BOON®
Hardback – January 2018

ROMANCE

Alexei's Passionate Revenge	Helen Bianchin
Prince's Son of Scandal	Dani Collins
A Baby to Bind His Bride	Caitlin Crews
A Virgin for a Vow	Melanie Milburne
Martinez's Pregnant Wife	Rachael Thomas
His Merciless Marriage Bargain	Jane Porter
The Innocent's One-Night Surrender	Kate Hewitt
The Consequence She Cannot Deny	Bella Frances
The Italian Billionaire's New Year Bride	Scarlet Wilson
The Prince's Fake Fiancée	Leah Ashton
Tempted by Her Greek Tycoon	Katrina Cudmore
United by Their Royal Baby	Therese Beharrie
Pregnant with His Royal Twins	Louisa Heaton
The Surgeon King's Secret Baby	Amy Ruttan
Forbidden Night with the Duke	Annie Claydon
Tempted by Dr Off-Limits	Charlotte Hawkes
Reunited with Her Army Doc	Dianne Drake
Healing Her Boss's Heart	Dianne Drake
The Rancher's Baby	Maisey Yates
Taming the Texan	Jules Bennett

MILLS & BOON®
Large Print – January 2018

ROMANCE

The Tycoon's Outrageous Proposal	Miranda Lee
Cipriani's Innocent Captive	Cathy Williams
Claiming His One-Night Baby	Michelle Smart
At the Ruthless Billionaire's Command	Carole Mortimer
Engaged for Her Enemy's Heir	Kate Hewitt
His Drakon Runaway Bride	Tara Pammi
The Throne He Must Take	Chantelle Shaw
A Proposal from the Crown Prince	Jessica Gilmore
Sarah and the Secret Sheikh	Michelle Douglas
Conveniently Engaged to the Boss	Ellie Darkins
Her New York Billionaire	Andrea Bolter

HISTORICAL

The Major Meets His Match	Annie Burrows
Pursued for the Viscount's Vengeance	Sarah Mallory
A Convenient Bride for the Soldier	Christine Merrill
Redeeming the Rogue Knight	Elisabeth Hobbes
Secret Lessons with the Rake	Julia Justiss

MEDICAL

The Surrogate's Unexpected Miracle	Alison Roberts
Convenient Marriage, Surprise Twins	Amy Ruttan
The Doctor's Secret Son	Janice Lynn
Reforming the Playboy	Karin Baine
Their Double Baby Gift	Louisa Heaton
Saving Baby Amy	Annie Claydon

MILLS & BOON®
Hardback – February 2018

ROMANCE

MILLS & BOON®
Large Print – February 2018

ROMANCE

Claimed for the Leonelli Legacy	Lynne Graham
The Italian's Pregnant Prisoner	Maisey Yates
Buying His Bride of Convenience	Michelle Smart
The Tycoon's Marriage Deal	Melanie Milburne
Undone by the Billionaire Duke	Caitlin Crews
His Majesty's Temporary Bride	Annie West
Bound by the Millionaire's Ring	Dani Collins
Whisked Away by Her Sicilian Boss	Rebecca Winters
The Sheikh's Pregnant Bride	Jessica Gilmore
A Proposal from the Italian Count	Lucy Gordon
Claiming His Secret Royal Heir	Nina Milne

HISTORICAL

Courting Danger with Mr Dyer	Georgie Lee
His Mistletoe Wager	Virginia Heath
An Innocent Maid for the Duke	Ann Lethbridge
The Viking Warrior's Bride	Harper St. George
Scandal and Miss Markham	Janice Preston

MEDICAL

Tempted by the Bridesmaid	Annie O'Neil
Claiming His Pregnant Princess	Annie O'Neil
A Miracle for the Baby Doctor	Meredith Webber
Stolen Kisses with Her Boss	Susan Carlisle
Encounter with a Commanding Officer	Charlotte Hawkes
Rebel Doc on Her Doorstep	Lucy Ryder

MILLS & BOON®

Why shop at millsandboon.co.uk?

Each year, thousands of romance readers find their perfect read at millsandboon.co.uk. That's because we're passionate about bringing you the very best romantic fiction. Here are some of the advantages of shopping at www.millsandboon.co.uk:

* **Get new books first**—you'll be able to buy your favourite books one month before they hit the shops

* **Get exclusive discounts**—you'll also be able to buy our specially created monthly collections, with up to 50% off the RRP

* **Find your favourite authors**—latest news, interviews and new releases for all your favourite authors and series on our website, plus ideas for what to try next

* **Join in**—once you've bought your favourite books, don't forget to register with us to rate, review and join in the discussions

Visit **www.millsandboon.co.uk** for all this and more today!

MILLS_WEB_HB